HUGO VON HOFMANNSTHAL

SELECT NARRATIVE PROSE

Hugo von Hofmannsthal

SELECT NARRATIVE PROSE

Translated with an Introduction
by Alexander Stillmark

Published by Ariadne Press, © 2020
Cover design and layout: Tim Lumsdaine
Front cover image: *Mondsee with Schafberg* by
Anatoly Kaigorodov, 1945
Back cover photograph of Hugo von Hofmannsthal:
Nicola Perscheid, 1910

Publisher's Cataloging in Publication Data
Names: Hofmannsthal, Hugo von, 1874-1929, author. |
Stillmark, Alexander, translator.
Title: Hugo von Hofmannsthal : select narrative prose /
translated with an introduction by Alexander Stillmark.
Series: Studies in Austrian Literature, Culture and
Thought. Translation series
Description: Riverside, CA: Ariadne Press, 2020.
Identifiers: ISBN 978-1-57241-211-8
Subjects: LCSH Hofmannsthal, Hugo von, 1874-1929.
| Hofmannsthal, Hugo von, 1874-1929--Criticism and
interpretation. | BISAC LITERARY COLLECTIONS /
European / General
Classification: LCC PT2617.O47 S413 2020 | DDC
832/.912 --dc23

HUGO VON HOFMANNSTHAL

SELECT NARRATIVE PROSE

TRANSLATED WITH AN INTRODUCTION
BY ALEXANDER STILLMARK

CONTENTS

INTRODUCTION

There is scarcely a modern writer more difficult to subsume under a single heading or category than Hugo von Hofmannsthal. His manifold gifts as a poet, playwright, librettist, novelist, essayist, anthologist and co-founder of the Salzburg Festival are astonishing enough. That he assimilated so much literary tradition while at the same time exploring a wealth of new forms such as lyrical drama, the prose poem or the fictional letter, gives his oeuvre an appearance of protean creativity. The twin forces of tradition and innovation are co-existent in him and both give impetus to his art.

Born in Vienna in 1874 and heir to the great legacy of European letters, he commanded the principal ancient and modern languages and as an avid reader was conversant with all major writers of the past. Vienna at the turn of the nineteenth century is to be seen as a focal meeting-place of European culture: it is the city of Gustav Mahler, Sigmund Freud, Ernst Mach, Gustav Klimt, Hermann Bahr, Arthur Schnitzler and Karl Kraus, to name but a few of the most prominent of the artists, writers and thinkers who lent distinction to that great centre of 'the multi-national state'. It was a city which continued to hold fast to tradition in its social and political life: it preserved its ancient monarchy until the death of Emperor Franz Joseph in 1916. Hofmannsthal saw forty-two years of that reign and had only eleven more years of life left after the new Republic of Austria was established in 1918.

At the turn of the century, Vienna was in the *avant-garde* of literature and the arts. The principal literary movements of Impressionism, Symbolism and Naturalism all vied with one another at this important transitional period. The period of 'Decadence', as it was later called, embraced numerous intellectual currents which contributed to an upsurge of a new aesthetic that involved experiment and attempts at new forms of expression. Prominent among these was 'Aestheticism' which proclaimed the pre-eminence of beauty, the self-sufficiency of art, the refinement of the sensibilities, a world-view which eschewed morality in art and fostered narcissism in the artist. 'Die Wiener Moderne' (the modern movement in Vienna) was the name given to this period between 1890 and 1910 which provided new creative impulses to literature and the arts and produced many works of lasting importance.

The young poet Hofmannsthal was a central figure in the Viennese literary scene of that time. He began to publish poems at the age of sixteen while still a scholar at the renowned Akademisches Gymnasium under the pen-name Loris, since publication by a minor was not permitted by law. Anyone reading his earliest poems and lyrical dramas will understand the incredulity and admiration which greeted the young poet when he was first introduced to the literary circles of Vienna in 1890. The prodigy called Loris was a sensation. At the Café Griensteidl, where leading literati regularly met to read from their manuscripts and exchange views, the schoolboy-poet was soon welcomed and accepted as a fellow artist. Arthur Schnitzler, his senior by some twelve years, noted in his diary in 1891: "Significant talent, a 17-year old boy Loris (v. Hofmannsthal). Knowledge, clarity and, it appears, also true artistic ability; unheard of at that age." The austere vatic poet Stefan George, who visited Vienna in the same year, also sought Hofmannsthal's acquaintance and wished to gain him as a contributor to his exclusive journal 'Blätter für die Kunst'. (The problematical relationship between these very different poets is a chapter in itself, no less than Hofmannsthal's ambivalent relations with Rilke. What matters is the important correspondence with each that resulted and which remains as a testimony to a meeting of minds involving the three foremost German poets of the age). Hofmannsthal's understanding of his role as a poet contrasts greatly with George's; for the latter chose exclusivity, disdained the wider public and wrote as a master for his disciples. Hofmannsthal was all too conscious of his common bond with humanity, always accentuated man's connectedness with the world, with society, with animate nature and the moral imperative. His poem 'The Prophet' depicts the unnatural, claustrophobic atmosphere of the poet as aesthete, encapsulated in an artificial realm which exerts an uncanny hypnotic influence on the senses. Here he rejects purely sensuous allurement, all sterile beauty which captivates like a spell, words which assert their unhealthy power over imagination and will. His early poetry is generally more intimate, life-affirming; it speaks with sensitive fellow-feeling of the destinies of all mankind, it stems from an inner sentient self, the well-spring of his moral being.

Hofmannsthal's early work is mainly lyrical; it is largely absorbed with exploration of the self, especially the creative self. He creates a great variety of 'Gestalten' or poetic personas which explore and body forth this focus of attention. The figures that stand out are Andrea (*Yesterday*), Claudio (*The Fool and Death*), Fortunio (*The White Fan*), Elis Fröböm (*The Mine at Falun*); all highly sensitive portraits which in different ways reflect facets of the artist or the artistic temperament set within the 'Zeitgeist' or temper of the age. This choice of invented personas owes much to the precedent of both Nikolaus Lenau and Robert Browning, whose penetrating dramatic monologues exploring individual psychology were greatly admired by Hofmannsthal. The condition of being a poet, with all the attendant problems, is reflected in myriad ways and fleshed out in these imagined portraits. The need to establish ties and lines of communication with living reality, to resist the lure of pure solipsism, of the magical beauty of words, of art for art's sake; that is the underlying tenor of his youthful oeuvre. Yet he was largely misunderstood as someone siding with the aesthetic movement and seen as an aesthete, a fellow-traveller of Pater, Wilde and Mallarmé. In his essay on Pater he wrote: "We are nearly all, in one way or another, in love with a past viewed and stylized through the medium of the arts. This is, so to speak, our manner of being in love with ideal or at least idealized life." But he was adamant in his rejection of aestheticism as a creed and wrote in exasperated self-defence: "Strange endlessly repeated reproach vis-à-vis my first products that they spring from an egoistic, aesthetic solitude, from an inhumane nature, devoid of sympathy. In *Yesterday* and *Death and the Fool* it is precisely something which addresses the discovery of a higher relationship to mankind." The encounter with George had made Hofmannsthal look with apprehension and disapproval on the poet who made a religion of his art and sealed it off from the problems and conflicts of human experience. He recognized the danger and was fully alive to the atmosphere of decadence which pervaded the *fin de siècle* generation. It was one of morbid hypersensitivity indulged in by a self-centered elite who cultivated aesthetic taste, sensibility and intellect but who put art before life and made life into a cult. He describes them in his essays on Swinburne and on Gabriele D'Annuncio: "One sometimes has the feeling, as though our fathers (the contemporaries of the younger Offenbach) had bequeathed to us late-born sons only two things: pretty furniture and hypersensitive nerves."

Though Hofmannsthal felt many affinities with "the dreamy-minded generation" as he called them, his early work already shows the problematical question of aesthetic self-indulgence, of losing contact with the realities and responsibilities of life by dwelling excessively in a world of beauty. Confrontation with the moral issue is a constant motif in the early work and it is this factor which introduces a significant element of tension and conflict. These early stirrings of the dramatic within the lyrical mode are not mere contrivances: they are rooted in the poet's moral consciousness and become increasingly prominent as he develops into a dramatist. The theme of death frequently enters into his writing. It is central to *The White Fan*, *The Death of Titian* and *Death and the Fool*, and prominent in poems such as 'Experience', 'Youth and the Spider', 'Idyll', 'Life'. The introduction of Death as an allegorical figure is especially effective in the lyrical drama *The Fool and Death*(1893) : a device which anticipates his later festival drama *Everyman*. For the central character Claudio it represents a confrontation with the moral self and the deepest sources of life, with the reality of being. Death is the messenger of new life. This profound paradox, which the nineteen year-old formulated in glowing verse, is a crucial moral insight vouchsafed the poet and offered as a riposte to the aesthetic movement. Claudio's name derives from the Latin 'claudere' to limp (vide the crippled emperor Claudius), only in him it is a moral disability which is being exposed. Claudio's vision of life, as expressed in the opening monologue, is wholly narcissistic; a glorying in his own aesthetic sensibilities since he sees not nature and man but painted landscapes and emotively drawn, idealized portraits. He has never had the capacity to feel, to experience the fullness of life as a reality. He has lived with borrowed emotions, surrogate experience, second-hand perceptions and insights. He has never been fully alive. Now Death comes to him not as a skeletal figure of finiteness, but rather as a Dionysian force, an admonisher, a harbinger of a newness of vision. He confronts Claudio with a moral insight into his squandered existence; he stirs in him for the first time presentiments of genuine love, friendship and sympathy. Death summons up three figures (the Mother, the Young Girl, the Man) which represent the closest of human bonds and each in turn calls to mind in Claudio the egotistical wasteland of his past life. Hofmannsthal depicts narcissism as a state of continual self-admiration; the hermetic condition of the aesthete who mirrors only himself in looking at things. He is a victim of his self-love, a prey to his own emotions and thoughts but blind to those of others. There is no truly valid outer world for the aesthete; everything consists only in received impression, sensation, appeal to the imagination. The play is a condemnation of such an existence; Claudio is judged by Death in no uncertain terms:

"You fool, you wicked fool, yet I shall teach you
For once to honour life, before you end it."

The moral confrontation with his former self leads Claudio to insight, though it comes too late since he cannot re-live his life. In his final words Claudio realizes that he cannot ultimately gain a victory over his accuser and that moral illumination must remain his sole reward: "Only now in dying, do I sense that I am." The realization that there is an intenser life of experience than any he had ever known is the final note. This lyrical drama presents a clear-sighted critique of the life-denying nature of aestheticism which Hofmannsthal had made his own almost from his earliest creative phase. His own path lay rather towards what he called "Weltfrömmigkeit", fervent affirmation of the world, wholehearted embracing of all experience not mere dalliance with formal beauty.

If *The Fool and Death* presented us with an une-quivocal verdict on the deadly consequences of the aesthetic life, *The Tale of the 672nd Night* (1895) offers a counter-piece with different accentuation but essentially on the same subject. "The basis of the Aesthetic is morality", Hofmannsthal had noted in 1893, just two years before he had written this work. The indispensable connection between the two concepts is demonstrated in the depiction of the merchant son: a modern Arabian Nights figure who exists in an illusory world of unsullied beauty surrounded by every luxury and pleasure, yet cut off in his walled garden from all knowledge of the outside world. His domain consists of untroubled and inviolate tranquillity; he believes it contains all the images and colours which constitute the myriad wonders of the world. He is intoxicated by the sheer variety and loveliness of his garden to the exclusion of all else. But there remains a gnawing doubt within him: "Yet he felt equally the nullity of all these things as well as their beauty; the thought of death never left him for long". This doubt as to the value of the things of beauty is the fundamental moral question underlying the merchant son's existence. This modern parable is an allegory of the aesthete's dream of perfection which is tested against an unresisting world and found to be wanting. The exotic setting, the dream-like atmosphere, the sensuous exploration of beauty and the intoxicating perfumed garden are correlatives of the alluring life of the aesthete at the *fin de siècle*. The setting owes some significant features to the influential novel *A Rebours* published by J-K. Huysmans in 1884. The labyrinthine development of the story, pursuing a pattern of adventure and strange encounters, seems to follow a predestined line; very much in the way a dream follows through to its inevitable conclusion. The secluded world of beauty is deserted for a brutal world of ugliness, squalor and pain. Recurrent images are used in a leitmotif-like manner to produce a line of associations and recollections; a technique clearly evocative of the dream. It hardly needs to be emphasized that Hofmannsthal is living and writing in the same city as Freud whose magnum opus *The Interpretation of Dreams* was first published in 1899.

The merchant son's gravitation towards death is as inevitable as it is mysterious; it is the fulfilment of his destiny, and again the death motif is used to highlight a decisive confrontation within the moral consciousness. Hofmannsthal's powers of graphic description in the agonized death of the merchant son amidst the squalor and ugliness of the lowest orders of society stand in blatant contrast to the opening of the work. Fear and pain are his last experience of life and he hates his own death as he curses the life that led to it. The parable of the beautiful life is transformed into the direst abhorrence; it is as if Hofmannsthal were showing in this harrowing conclusion that he could write as powerfully in a thoroughly realistic vein as any contemporary Naturalist.

The art displayed in Hofmannsthal's early poetry shows an amazing maturity and control; every word is fitted with an unerring sureness of touch. The universal symbolism encapsulated in the simple form of a poem such as 'Die Beiden' (He and She) carries the full imprint of the poet's style; it is a symbolic style which was to persist and grow to find ever broader subjects and new forms throughout his creative life. Hofmannsthal was deeply aware of his poetic genius and vocation and constantly monitored the creative process. In 1904 he noted in his diary: "I am a poet because I experience figuratively". In another telling reflection he noted: "All that exists, Being and Meaning, is one; consequently all Being is Symbol." It was not just to the French Symbolists (Baudelaire, Verlaine, Rimbaud) that he owed his developed sense of figurative language and the universality of symbolic statement, but to the early German Romantic Novalis. Symbol and metaphor may be said to become for him almost a mode of apprehension. The facility for thinking in metaphor distinguishes not only the young Hofmannsthal but is an indissoluble part of his creative use of language. The reflections he published under the heading "Figurative Expression" (1897) contain some of his fundamental convictions about the symbolic nature of literature and are close to Novalis both in spirit and in form, e.g.: "Core and nature of all poetry: every work of literature is essentially and throughout a construct of figurative expressions." From youth to maturity the conviction remains that the province of poetry is symbolism and that the poet's natural mode of expression is "in unending parables".

The influence of Novalis may variously be traced in the early essays and reflections but particularly in *A Letter* (1902); a fictive letter from a young writer, Lord Chandos, to his friend and mentor Sir Francis Bacon.

This essay is among the most representative writings of the age and immediately caught the attention of Hofmannsthal's fellow artists. For many it constituted the crucial expression of the modern writer's dilemma as it formulated through penetrating self-scrutiny both an agonizing doubt and a newness of vision. Chandos has reached a crisis in that he finds language simply inadequate as a vehicle of self-expression or communication. For him words have lost coherence and meaning; they can no longer express or convey wholeness of perception and experience: "My case is briefly this: I have totally lost the capacity to think or to speak coherently about anything whatsoever." The loss of coherence, of the connectedness of things, the loss of control over meaning, the loss of unity or harmony, the questioning of fundamental concepts such as 'mind', 'soul' or 'body' – all this overwhelms him and leaves him without an answer. Chandos hardly finds himself to be the same person that he was the previous day. He is beset by the deepest doubts which are both existential and verbal, so that a great chasm seems to have opened up between the sphere of experience and that of language. This 'malady of my mind' as he calls it, involves every faculty: reason, logic, perception, intuition and sensibility. The great sense of oneness with the universe he had once possessed seems irretrievably lost. Hofmannsthal is of course, intimately involved in this searching out of the roots of an intellectual crisis and he has recourse to the language of metaphor in attempting to express the complexity of his quest for meaning. The desire for restitution of a lost unity is at the centre of *A*

Letter and it is especially made present in the phrase "to think with our heart" which Chandos proposes as a possible means of entering into fuller communion with all being. The language of the letter, which is full of striking metaphor, simile and symbolism, is itself an attempt to fuse the conceptual with the sensuous and experiential.

The glorious paradox of the Chandos letter is that it represents language at its most penetrating, vital and illuminating. Hofmannsthal had formulated the crisis which he and other writers of the modern age had encountered and in doing so had actually surmounted it. Chandos finds a new, intenser form of meaning communicated to him through a variety of encounters with objects, animals and scenes which inwardly deeply stir him. These epiphanies are the "moments of heightened experience" which the poet needs and values most. They are flashes of insight and inspiration; discrete, unexpected and overpowering in their force: "the source of that mysterious, wordless, boundless rapture". The experience that lies beyond words can only be articulated by the poet: in ruminating on this mysterious phenomenon and offering us a last example Chandos-Hofmannsthal comes to use an expression which transcends the bounds of common experience: "a kind of feverish thinking, but thinking within a material which is more immediate, more liquid, more glowing than words." Hofmannsthal indeed soon moved from the lyrical to the dramatic genre and went on to extend his range in prose and verse. After writing the tragedy *Elektra* (1903), which became his first libretto for Richard Strauss, he approached music as the perfect complement to the word, and his collaboration with the composer lasted to the end of his life, producing some of the finest libretti ever written such as *Der Rosenkavalier*, *Die Frau ohne Schatten*, and *Arabella*.

The principal direction in Hofmannsthal's development after *A Letter* lay towards the drama as he now embarked on a number of classical subjects (*Everyman*, *Orestes*, *Oedipus*, the *Bacchae*). At the same time he turned to prose forms (the unfinished novel *Andreas*) and continued to write essays and imaginative prose. The short stories or Novellen which he wrote between 1895 and 1900, and included in this collection, are widely considered as his finest contribution to the genre. They are generally impressionistic in style and are remarkable for their searching psychological interest as they feel out the inner life of each leading character. In the case of *Cavalry Tale* Hofmannsthal offers us a memorable instance of what in Freudian terms is called déjà vu when Sergeant Lech encounters his double in an ominous scene. In adapting a short story by Goethe (Experience of Marshal Bassompierre) and subtly expanding its subject into a symbolic exploration of the themes of erotic passion and death, Hofmannsthal pays tribute to the poet he revered and looked back to more than any other. The delightful short story *Lucidor*, written in light ironic vein, shows us the poet's sovereign capacity for treating a comic subject. Indeed it is the blueprint for the libretto of Arabella, the late opera which concluded his collaboration with Strauss and which only came out in 1929, the year in which he died.

Hofmannsthal's abiding concern as a creative artist was with the medium of language; to him language was the repository of his culture, the vital carrier of tradition. His faith in the unbroken continuum of language and form as the vital element of the practicing artist, this "vertical thinking" as he once called it, is a fundamental tenet. His traditionalism is largely to be understood in terms of a deep attachment to the life-giving potency of form. His recognition of the form-conscious Austrian tradition of literature from Grillparzer onwards is of a piece with this thinking. "The old and the new is present side by side, it is truly a little more present with us than elsewhere", he wrote in his essay "Austria in the Mirror of its Literature". He saw Grillparzer as the perfect blend of tradition and innovation and believed that Austrian culture, through its central European location, played a mediatory role between East and West. His receptivity towards the major traditions of the western world is a testimony to the Goethean concept of "Weltliteratur", i.e. to the notion of literature as a universal, undivided cultural legacy to which national traditions are subordinate and with which they fruitfully interact. Hofmannsthal was drawn to all great periods of literature: classical antiquity, Renaissance, Elizabethan, Baroque or European Classicism, without limitation to any one nation; yet one abiding focus of interest proved to be the allegorical mystery play, and here he made lasting contributions to the stage with *Everyman*, *The Salzburg Great World Theatre* and *The Tower*. His collaboration with Max Reinhardt, the leading theatrical director of the day, gave rise to the founding of the Salzburg Festival in 1922 where *Everyman* is annually performed outside the cathedral. While preserving the formal elements of the *teatrum mundi*, and creating a poetic language which skilfully blends historical features of style with the contemporary language, the effect achieved is that of a drama of timeless significance in which fundamental problems of a moral and religious kind are enacted. Hofmannsthal was more concerned to create in drama an "atmosphere of the present" in which contemporary man could find himself, than to transmit a sense of the historical past. In reviving the medieval morality play he demonstrated how the simple allegories of the past could be made present and meaningful to modern audiences.

Hofmannsthal not only excelled in tragic and allegorical drama; his engagement with comic theatre was also a life-long undertaking. He even called his earliest play *Yesterday* an "embryo of the poetisized social comedy". In his view comedy was not founded merely on the virtuosic deployment of language which entertains by its wit and levity, but it was essentially a social form. The configurations of society, the interaction between members of society, were comic material *per se*: "People in relation to people are simply always comical." The contrasts and conflicts which come into play by introducing a mixed social gathering were sufficient in themselves to produce the effect of irony; and this he saw as the basic element of comedy. In his comedies he exhibits a refined sense of the uses of irony when employed as a vehicle for the exploration of a social scene. He did not resort to the exaggerations or distortions on which satire depends, though his portrayal of character is not without critical acumen. His finest achievement in the genre of comedy is, by general critical acclaim, "Der Schwierige" (*An Impossible Man*). Published in 1921 and first performed in Munich in the same year, the comedy has established itself as a modern classic. Some of the poet's friends saw the central figure Hans Karl (defined by his creator as "the refined, clever Viennese") as self-portrayal. The problematical relationship to language as a theme in the play may indeed recall much that the famous "Chandos Letter" had addressed in the past, but the dramatist's skill in creating a complex and objective stage figure supervenes. Hans Karl clearly stands in the tradition of Molière's "Le Misanthrope" and in creating his masterpiece Hofmannsthal had shown himself to be a keen critical reader of that genius of comedy.

Hofmannsthal left a considerable legacy of writing to posterity; a good many fragments and sketches remained, yet nothing to compare with the great volume of completed works. His death on 15th July 1929 was sudden and tragic: he suffered a stroke as he was setting out to attend the funeral of his son Franz who had ended his own life. Thousands attended the poet's funeral. Arthur Schnitzler made this entry in his diary: "The greatest poet of the age has vanished with him."

A.S.

TALE OF THE 672nd NIGHT

A young merchant's son who was very handsome and had neither father nor mother, soon after his twenty-fifth birthday had grown tired of the convivial life of wining and dining. He closed off most of the rooms in his house and dismissed all but four of his male and female servants whose loyalty and entire nature were dear to him. Since he cared little for his friends and not a single woman's beauty so captivated him as to make it seem desirable or merely tolerable to have her always about him, he accustomed himself ever more to a fairly solitary life which seemed to correspond closest to his state of mind. Yet he was by no means unsociable, but on the contrary would happily go for walks in the streets or public gardens and look intently on people's faces. Neither did he neglect the care of his body and his beautiful hands, nor the décor of his home. Indeed the beauty of his carpets, tapestries and silks, of the carved and panelled walls, of candelabra and basins made of metal, of glass and earthenware vessels, took on a significance for him which he had never dreamed of. Gradually he developed an eye for how all forms and colours of the world were alive in his garden. He discerned in the convolutions of ornaments an enchanted image of the convoluted marvels of the world. He found the forms of animals and the forms of flowers and the transition of flowers into animals; the dolphins, lions and tulips, the pearls and acanthus; he found the conflict between the gravity of pillars and the resistance of firm ground and the upward thrust of all water and again its downward fall; he found the bliss of motion and the sublimity of repose, of dance and of the state of death; he found the colours of flowers and foliage, the colours of wild creatures and the faces of nations, the colours of gemstones, the colour of the stormy and the calm gleam of the sea; yes, he found the moon and the stars, the mystic orb, the mystic rings and firmly grafted to them, the wings of the seraphim. For a long time he was intoxicated by this great, profound beauty which belonged to him, and all his days continued lovelier and less empty amongst these objects which were no longer something dead and base but rather a great heritage, the divine work of all generations.

Yet he felt equally the nullity of all these things as well as their beauty; the thought of death never left him for long and it often sought him out amongst laughing, boisterous people, often at night, often during meals.

But since he harboured no illness, the thought held no terrors but rather contained something of solemnity and splendour and appeared most forcefully when thinking beautiful thoughts or the beauty of his youth and solitude most enthralled him. For the merchant son drew great pride from the mirror, from the verses of poets, from his wealth and his intelligence and gloomy proverbs did not burden his soul. He said: "wherever you are to die, your feet will carry you", and saw himself as beautiful, like a king lost whilst hunting, moving towards a strange, marvellous destiny in an unfamiliar forest amongst strange trees. He said: "when the house is complete, then death will come," and he saw the latter's slow advance across the palace bridge supported by winged lions, to the completed house loaded with the wonderful spoils of life.

He imagined that he lived in complete solitude but his four servants encircled him like dogs and even though he spoke very little with them, he somehow sensed that they constantly thought to serve him well. He too began to think about them at one time or another.

The housekeeper was an old woman; her deceased daughter had been the merchant son's wet-nurse; all her other children had died. She was very silent and the chill of old age went out from her white face and her white hands. But he liked her since she had always been in the house and since recollection of his own mother's voice and of his childhood, which he loved and yearned for, went about with her.

She had taken a distant relative into the house, with his permission, who was scarcely fifteen years old who was most reserved. She was harsh towards herself and hard to understand. Once, on a dark and sudden impulse of her angry soul, she threw herself from a window into the yard but with her childlike body fell upon garden soil which had by chance been heaped up, so that she only broke a collar-bone because a stone had stuck in the earth there. Once she had been brought to bed, the merchant son sent a doctor to her; in the evening, however, he himself came to see how she was. She kept her eyes closed and for a long time he looked at her calmly for the first time and was astonished at the strange and precocious gracefulness of her face. Only her lips were very thin and in that there lay something ugly and uncanny. Suddenly

HUGO VON HOFMANNSTHAL

she opened her eyes, looked at him with an icy and angry glance and with lips compressed in anger, mastering her pain, turned to the wall so that she came to lie upon her wounded side. Instantly her deathly pale face discoloured to greenish white, she fainted and fell back as though dead into her former posture.

When she had recovered her health the merchant son did not speak to her for a long while whenever she crossed his path. On a few occasions he asked the old woman if the girl did not like being in his house, but she always denied it. The only servant he had decided to retain in his house, he had come to know when one evening he had dined at the ambassador's, whom the King of Persia was entertaining in that town. This man had saved him then and had shown such helpfulness and solicitude and appeared to have such self-constraint and modesty that the merchant son took greater pleasure in observing him than in the conversation of all the other guests. All the greater was his joy when, many months later, this same servant approached him in the street, greeted him with the same deep seriousness and lack of importunity as on that past evening and offered his services. The merchant son at once recognized him by his mulberry-coloured face and his very good manners. He at once took him into his service, dismissed two young servants still employed by him and thereafter let himself be waited on at meals and otherwise solely by this serious and reserved man. This man hardly ever made use of the permission to leave the house in the evening hours. He showed a rare form of devotedness to his master, whose wishes he anticipated and whose likes and dislikes he tacitly surmised, so that the master too felt an ever growing attachment to him.

Even when he allowed himself to be served only at table by him, a maidservant would bring him dishes filled with fruit and sweet pastries; a young girl, yet nonetheless a year or two older than the little girl. This young girl was one who would hardly be judged a beauty if one saw her from a distance by torchlight since then the subtler features are lost; but as he saw her daily and close by, he was deeply moved by the matchless beauty of her eyelids and her lips, and the languid, cheerless motion of her lovely figure struck him as the mysterious language of an inaccessible and marvellous world.

Whenever the heat of summer in town was very great and the torrid glow hovered along the houses, or on sultry, heavy, full-moon nights the wind drove white dust clouds through empty streets, the merchant son set off with his servants for a country house he possessed in the mountains, set in a narrow valley surrounded by dark peaks. Waterfalls cascaded into the depths from both sides, which provided coolness. The moon almost always stood behind the mountains but great white clouds rose high over the black walls, drifted solemnly across the dark, gleaming sky and vanished on the other side. Here the merchant son lived his customary life in a house whose wooden walls were constantly refreshed by the cool fragrance of gardens and numerous waterfalls. In the afternoon he would sit in his garden until the sun sank down behind the mountains and mostly read a book in which the wars of some mighty king of the past were recorded. Sometimes he would stop suddenly amidst a description where the thousand horsemen of hostile kings turned back their mounts screaming, or where their war chariots had plunged down the steep bank of a river, since he sensed without looking up that the eyes of his four servants were fixed on him. He knew without raising his head that they looked at him without saying a word, each one from a different room. He knew them so well. He felt them live, stronger, more urgently than he felt himself alive. About himself he sometimes sensed some slight emotion or surprise, yet on this account a curious oppression. He felt with nightmarish clarity how the two elderly ones were moving towards their death with every hour, through the remorseless, gentle alteration of their features and their gestures which he knew so well; and how the two girls were drifting into that desolate, some-how airless life. For him the dead weight of their life, of which they themselves were oblivious, burdened his very limbs like the horror and deathly bitterness of a terrible dream which is forgotten on awakening.

At times he had to rise and walk about so as not to succumb to this fear. But while he gazed upon the lurid gravel at his feet and with keenest concentration dwelt on how the smell of carnations wafted up to him in light breaths from the cool smell of grass and earth and mingled with the smell of heliotrope in mild, over-sweet clouds, he felt their eyes and could think of nothing else. Without raising his head he knew that the old crone sat at her window, her bloodless hands resting on the sun-drenched ledge, her bloodless mask-like face an ever more horrendous home for those helpless black eyes that could not die away. Without lifting her head he sensed when the servant stepped back from his window for a few minutes and busied himself at a cupboard; without looking up he awaited in secret fear the moment he would return. While with both hands he let supple branches close up behind him so as to hide himself away in the most overgrown corner of the garden, he urged all his thoughts towards the beauty of the heavens which sank down from above in small lustrous fragments of damp turquoise through the dark tangle of twigs and branches, his entire blood and thinking was captured solely by the knowledge that the two girls' eyes were fixed on him. Those of the bigger girl were weary and sad with a vague challenge that tormented him, those of the smaller with an impatient and yet mocking attentiveness which tormented him still more. And yet he never entertained the idea that they looked at him directly; himself, as he strolled about with bowed head or knelt down beside a carnation so as to bind it with bast, or bent beneath the branches. He felt rather, that they were observing his entire life, his deepest being, his secret, human insufficiency.

He was seized by a terrible anxiety, a deadly fear of the inescapability of life. More terrible than their incessant observation of him was the fact that they impelled him in so fruitless and wearisome a manner to think of himself. And the garden was far too small to escape them. But when he was very close by them, his fear vanished so completely that he almost forgot past experience. He was then able to ignore them completely or calmly to observe their movements, which were so familiar that he derived from them a constant, as it were, bodily sympathy for their lives.

The little girl only encountered him now and then on the stairs or in the hallway. The other three, however, were frequently with him in the same room.

Once he caught sight of the bigger girl in a tilted mirror; she was walking through an adjacent room that was raised, but within the mirror she approached him from the deeper background. She moved slowly and with an effort but quite erect: in each arm she carried a heavy, gaunt Indian deity made of dark bronze. She held the decorated feet of the figures in hollow hands; the dark goddesses reached from her hips to her forehead and leaned their dead weight against her vital, delicate shoulders. But the dark heads with their wicked mouths filled with snakes, three wild eyes in each forehead and uncanny jewellery in their cold, hard hair, moved alongside those breathing cheeks and brushed the lovely temples in time with her slow strides. Yet in fact she did not seem to feel the solemn burden of the goddesses, but rather that of the beauty of her own head with its weighty adornment of dark, living gold, two large rounded plaits to either side of her bright brow, just like a warrior queen. He was deeply moved by her great beauty but at the same time knew for certain that it would mean nothing to him to hold her in his arms. He knew all in all that his servant's beauty filled him with yearning but not with desire, so that he did not let his eyes rest on her for long but left the room, indeed stepped out into the street and continued in strange disquiet along the narrow shade between the houses and gardens. Finally he approached the river bank where gardeners and florists lived and – even though he knew he sought in vain – looked long for a flower's form and fragrance, or for a spice whose transient waft might momentarily offer him that sweet charm of calm possession which lay in his maidservant's beauty and which so perplexed and disturbed him. And while he sought in vain with longing eyes in the sultry hot-houses or bent over long flower beds out of doors where the light was already fading, his brain involuntarily, at last tormented and against his will, repeated the poet's lines: "Amongst the stems of carnations swaying, in the fragrance of ripened corn, you aroused my yearning; but once I found you, it was not you I found, but your soul's sister."

II

In the course of these days there came a letter which in some measure disturbed his mind. The letter was unsigned. The writer accused the merchant son's servant in vague terms of having committed some abominable crime or other in the house of his former master, the Persian ambassador. This unknown person appeared to harbour fierce hatred against the servant and added many threats; he also adopted an impolite, almost threatening tone towards the merchant son himself. But it was impossible to guess what kind of crime was being insinuated and what purpose, if any, this letter might have for the writer who did not give his name and made no demands. He read the letter several times and told himself that he felt great fear at the thought of losing his servant in so repulsive a manner. The more he thought about it, the more he was aroused, and the less he could endure the thought of losing one of these beings with whom he had through force of habit and other secret powers fully grown together.

He strode up and down and his furied agitation so inflamed him that he threw off his jacket and belt and stamped on them. He felt as though his innermost possession was being insulted and threatened and he was being forced to flee from himself and to deny what was dear to him. He pitied himself and, as was usual in these instances, sensed himself a child. He already saw his four servants torn from his home and he imagined that the entire content of his life were silently oozing out of him, all painfully sweet memories, all half-conscious expectations, everything inexpressible, only to be cast out somewhere and rejected as worthless just like a clump of algae and seaweed. He realized for the first time what had always incited him to anger as a small boy; the anxious love with which his father clung to what he had amassed, to the treasures of his vaulted warehouse, the secret figments of the dark and deepest desires of his heart. He realized that the great king of past ages would have to die if he had been deprived of those lands which he had crossed and conquered from the sea in the West to the sea in the East; lands which he dreamed of ruling and yet were so infinitely vast that he had no power over them and received no tribute from them save the thought that he had subjected them and that he alone was king and no one but himself.

He resolved to do everything to put this matter, which troubled him so greatly, to rest. Without telling the servant a word about the letter, he got ready and set out alone for the city. There he decided first to seek out the house where the ambassador to the King of Persia resided; for he harboured a vague hope of somehow finding there a lead of some kind.

However, when he arrived it was late in the afternoon and no one was at home, neither the ambassador nor one of the young members of his entourage. Only the cook and an old subordinate clerk were sitting in the gateway in the cool semi-darkness. But they were so ugly and gave such curt, grumpy replies that he impatiently turned his back on them and decided to come back next day at a more favourable time.

Since his own house was now locked up – for he had left no servant behind in the town – he had to think in terms of a stranger how to find a night's lodging for himself. Curious, like a stranger, he walked through the familiar streets and at last reached the banks of a small stream which had all but dried up in this season. From there he walked lost in thought along a somewhat squalid street where a great many prostitutes lived. Without paying much attention to the direction he was taking, he then turned right and entered a completely deserted, deathly calm cul-de-sac which ended in a steep towering stairway. He came to a halt on the steps and looked back on his path. He could look down into the backyards of the little houses; here and there red curtains were to be seen at the windows and ugly, dust-covered flowers. The broad, dry river-bed had something of a deathly sadness. He rose higher and at the top arrived at a quarter he could not recollect ever having seen. Nonetheless it suddenly seemed to him there was something familiar, in a dream-like way, about a lower street crossing. He carried on and came to a jeweller's shop. It was a very mean little shop, suited for this part of town, and the window was stocked with such valueless items of jewellery as may be purchased from pawnbrokers and receivers. The merchant son, who was well versed in precious gems, could scarcely find a single stone that was halfway beautiful.

Suddenly his eye lighted on a piece of old-fashioned jewellery made of fine gold, decorated with a beryl, which somehow reminded him of the old woman. He had probably once seen a similar piece on her at a time when she was a young woman. It also seemed to him that the pale, somewhat melancholy stone was in some way suited to her age and appearance; and the old-fashioned setting had the same kind of sadness. So he entered the humble shop so as to buy the jewellery. The jeweller was very pleased to see so well-dressed a customer enter and wished to further show him more precious gems which he did not display in the window. Out of politeness towards the old man, he let himself be shown many an object, but neither felt inclined to buying more nor could he think of any use for such presents in his solitary life. In the end he grew impatient and at the same time embarrassed, for he wished to break off and yet not offend the old man. He decided on buying another trifle and then to leave at once. Over the jeweller's shoulder he gazed without thought at a small silver hand-mirror which was half clouded. Thereupon there appeared out of another interior mirror the image of the young girl with the dark heads of the bronze goddesses to either side; he felt fleetingly that much of her charm lay in the way her shoulders and her hair bore the beauty of her head with humble, child-like grace: the head of a young queen. And fleetingly he thought it pretty to see a fine golden chain about that neck; wound multiple times round and yet reminiscent of armour. And he asked to see such chains. The old man opened a door and asked him to enter a second room, a low sitting room, but where many more articles of jewellery were displayed in glass cases and on open stands. He soon found a little chain here that he liked and then asked the jeweller to let him know the price of the two articles. The old man further asked him to take stock of the notable antique saddles fitted with semi-precious stones, but he replied, being a merchant's son, that he had never concerned himself with horses, indeed that he could not even ride and took no pleasure in either old or new saddles. He paid for what he had bought with a gold piece and several silver coins and showed some impatience at leaving the shop. While the old man, without a further word, selected a lovely sheet of tissue paper and wrapped the little chain and the beryl jewellery separately, the merchant son chanced to step up to the low, latticed window and looked out. He glimpsed a very well kept vegetable garden, evidently belonging to the neighbouring house, the background to which was formed by two glass-houses and a high wall. He was at once keen to see the glass-houses and asked the jeweller if he could show him the way there. The jeweller handed him his two little parcels and led him through an adjacent room into the yard which was connected with the neighbouring garden by means of a little latticed gate. Here the jeweller paused and knocked on the lattice with an iron clapper. But as everything remained silent in the garden, and nothing stirred in the neighbouring house, he suggested to the merchant son simply to go and view the hot-houses and should he be bothered by anyone, to refer them to him as one well acquainted with the owner of the garden. He then opened up for him by thrusting his hand through the grating. The merchant son at once moved along the wall to the nearest glass-house and found such an array of rare and striking narcissi and anemones and such strange foliage never yet seen by him, that he could not satisfy his eyes for a long while. At last he looked up and noticed that the sun had set behind the houses without his having noticed it. He did not now wish to remain in a strange, unsupervised garden but merely to cast a glance through the panes of another hot-house and then depart. As he walked, peering like this, past the glass walls of the second hot-house, he gave a great start and sprang back. For some person had pressed a face against the panes and was looking at him. A moment later he calmed down and became conscious that it was a child, a little girl no more than four years old at most whose white dress and pallid face were pressed against the panes. But as he looked closer, he gave another start with an unpleasant sensation of horror at the back of the neck and a slight tightening of the throat and deeper down his chest. For the child that gazed on him with a fixed, evil look in some inexplicable way resembled the five-year-old girl he kept in his house. Everything was alike, the light-coloured eyebrows, the fine trembling wings of the nostrils, the thin lips; like the other, this child also hunched up its shoulders a little. Everything was alike, only with this child all this made an impression which caused him dread. He did not know what lay behind his nameless fear. He only knew that he would not be able to bear it if he turned round and knew that this face was staring at him through the panes from behind.

In his fear he moved rapidly towards the glass-house door so as to enter; the door was closed and bolted from the outside; he stooped for the bolt which was very low, drew it back so violently that he painfully strained a tendon of his little finger and approached the child almost at a run. The child moved towards him without saying a word, thrust itself against his knees and tried to push him out with its weak little hands. He found it hard not to kick it. But his fear lessened through closeness. He bent down over the child's face, which was quite pale and whose eyes trembled from anger and hate, whilst the little teeth of its lower jaw pressed against the upper lip with an uncanny fury. His fear vanished for an instant and he stroked the little girl's short, fine hair. But in that instant he recalled the hair of the little girl in his house which he had once touched as she lay, deathly pale, with eyes closed in her bed, and all at once he again felt a cold shudder down his back, and he withdrew his hands. She had given up the attempt to push him out. She took a few steps back and looked straight ahead. The sight of this feeble little doll's body within its little white dress and the contemptuous, horrific, pale little child's face became all but unbearable to him. He was so filled with horror that he felt a pang within his temples and throat, as his hand brushed against something cold in his pocket. It was just a few silver coins. He took them out and let them fall at his feet so that they vanished through a crack in the ground covered by a grating of floor-boards. Then she turned her back on him and went out. He stood motionless for some time and his heart beat rapidly from fear that she would return and look at him through the panes from outside. He would have liked to leave at once but felt it better to let some time pass so that the child left the garden. By now it was no longer daylight in the glass-house and the shapes of the plants began to appear strange. At some distance away in the half darkness, black, meaningless, threatening branches began to stand out and beyond them something white shimmered, as though the child were standing there. Some pots with waxen flowers stood in a row upon a shelf. To deaden the passage of time a little he counted the blossoms which in their rigidness were quite unlike living flowers and seemed like masks, invidious masks whose eye-holes had sealed up. Once he was ready he moved towards the door and wanted to get out. The door did not yield; the child had bolted it from outside. He wanted to shout but feared his own voice. He hammered with his fists against the panes. The garden and the house remained deathly calm. Only at his back something slid rustling through the shrubs. He told himself that they were leaves which had loosened and fallen through vibration of the stuffy air. Just the same, he ceased his knocking and tried to pierce the half dark-ened tangle of trees and climbers with his glance. Then he glimpsed something like a square in dark outline on the dusky rear wall. He crawled forward, by now quite unconcerned if he crushed many earthenware pots and the tall thin stems and rustling fern tips collapsed above and behind him in ghostly manner. The square of dark outlines was the silhouette of a door and it yielded to his touch. The fresh air fanned his face; behind him he could hear the cracked stems and trodden-down leaves quietly rise again with rustling sounds as though after a thunderstorm.

He was standing in a narrow brick-lined passage; overhead the open sky looked down and the wall to either side was scarcely the height of a man. But the passage was once more bricked up after a distance of some fifteen paces, and once more he believed himself to be imprisoned. Irresolutely he passed on; there on the right the wall had been broken through to the width of a man and from the aperture a plank ran through the empty space across to a platform opposite; the latter was closed off on the facing side by a low iron grating, backed on the other two by tall occupied buildings. At the point where the plank rested like a boarding bridge on the platform edge, the grating had a little door.

So great was the merchant son's impatience to escape from the realm of his fear, that he at once set one foot after the other upon the plank, and with eyes fixed firmly on the opposite shore, he began to cross. Yet, unhappily, he still grew conscious that he was suspended above a deep, walled trench many stories high; he sensed fear and helplessness in the soles of his feet and the hollow of his knees; dizzy throughout his entire frame he sensed the nearness of death. He knelt down and closed his eyes; then his arms, in feeling forward, touched the bars of the grating. He clung to them firmly, they yielded, and with a light grinding sound which cut through him like the first kiss of death, there opened towards him, towards the abyss, the door he clung to; and caught up in a feeling of inner exhaustion and great dejection he already felt the smooth iron bars slipping from his fingers – they seemed the fingers of a child – as he plunged down and shattered against the wall. But the gentle opening of the door stopped before his feet had missed the plank and with a lunge he threw his trembling body through the opening and onto the hard ground.

He could not rejoice; with a dull sensation like hatred against the futility of these torments, he entered one of the houses, went down the shabby staircase and stepped once more into a back-street that looked ugly and vulgar. But he was already very sad and tired out and could think of nothing that gave grounds for any kind of joy. Everything had strangely fallen from him and he walked along this street, then the next and the next, completely empty and forsaken by life. He pursued one direction of which he knew that it would lead him back to that place in the city where the rich lived and where he might find shelter for the night. For he felt great longing for a bed. He recalled, with childlike delight, the beauty of his own bed, and there also came to his mind the beds which the great king of past ages had set up for himself and his daughters when they celebrated weddings with the daughters of conquered kings; a bed made of gold for himself, one of silver for the others; all supported on gryphons and winged bulls. Meanwhile he had arrived at the low dwellings where soldiers lived. He paid no heed to this. A few soldiers with sallow faces and sad eyes were sitting by a latticed window and called out something to him. He then raised his head and breathed in the musty smell which drifted out of the room, a smell that was singularly stifling. But he did not understand what they wanted of him. But since they had roused him out of his listless, aimless rambling, he now looked into the yard as he was passing the gateway. The yard was very large and sad and since it was growing dark it appeared even larger and sadder. There were also very few people in it, and the houses which surrounded it were low and of a dirty yellow colour. This made it seem even more desolate and larger. At one spot some twenty horses in a straight line were casually tethered to a post; in front of each knelt a soldier dressed in a stable-smock of coarse dirty linen who was washing its hooves. At quite some distance several others approached in pairs through a gate dressed in similar coarse linen outfits. They walked slowly, dragging their feet, and carried heavy sacks on their shoulders. Only when they came closer he could see that there was bread in the open sacks which they were lugging in dumb silence. He watched as they slowly vanished in a gateway and trudged on as though beneath an ugly, mean burden and carried their bread in sacks such as those in which the sadness of their bodies were wrapped.

He then went over to those who were kneeling in front of their horses and washing their hooves. These too resembled one another and were like those by the window and those who had carried bread. They must have come from neighbouring villages. They too scarcely exchanged a word amongst themselves. As it grew very difficult for them to hold the horse's front foot, their heads swayed and their tired, sallow faces rose and fell as though beneath strong wind. Most of the horses' heads were ugly and wore a malicious expression through ears laid back and curled up lips which exposed the upper canine teeth. They also had mostly wicked, rolling eyes and a strange way of snorting impatiently and disdainfully through contorted nostrils. The last horse in the row was especially powerful and ugly. It was trying to bite the man's shoulder with its great teeth as he knelt before it and dried off the washed hoof. The man had such hollow cheeks and such a deathly sad expression in his tired eyes that the merchant son was overwhelmed by deep, bitter sympathy. He wanted to cheer the miserable wretch for a moment by some gift and groped in his pocket for silver coins. He found none and remembered that he had wanted to offer the last ones to the child in the glasshouse, which she had scattered at his feet with such a malicious glance. He wanted to look for a gold coin since he had pocketed seven or eight of them for his journey.

At that moment the horse turned its head and looked at him with maliciously laid back ears and rolling eyes that appeared all the more malicious and ferocious since a blaze ran at eye-level right across its ugly head. At this ugly spectacle he recalled in a flash a long-forgotten human face. However hard he tried, he was incapable of recalling the features of this person; but now they were there. The memory that accompanied the face, however, was not so clear. He only knew that it stemmed from the time when he was twelve; a time somehow bound up with memories of the smell of sweet, warm, shelled almonds.

And he knew that it was the contorted face of an ugly, poor person whom he had seen just once in his father's shop. And that his face was contorted with fear, because other people threatened him, since he possessed a large gold coin and would not say where he had obtained it.

While this face again faded away, his fingers continued to search the folds of his clothing and when a sudden, passing thought arrested him, he withdrew his hand indecisively and in doing so, cast the jewellery with the beryl wrapped in tissue paper under the horse's feet. He stooped and the horse lashed out sideways with its hoof, kicking him with all its might in the loins and he fell on his back. He moaned aloud, his knees drawn upwards, and kept on striking the ground with his heels. A few of the soldiers rose and lifted him by his shoulders and under his knees. He took in the smell of their clothes, the same stuffy, desolate smell that had previously drifted onto the street from their room, and tried to recollect where, in times long past, he had ever breathed the like: at this his senses left him. They bore him away across a narrow stairs, through a long, mostly dark passage into one of their rooms and laid him down on a low, iron bed. They then searched his clothes, took from him the little chain and the seven gold coins and finally left him, moved to pity by his incessant moaning, to fetch one of their surgeons.

After a time he opened his eyes and grew conscious of his tormenting pain. But he was still more shocked and frightened at being alone in this desolate room. With great effort he turned his eyes in their painful sockets towards the wall and noticed on a shelf three such loaves of bread as they had carried across the yard.

Otherwise nothing else was in the room other than

hard, low beds and the smell of dried rushes, with which the beds were stuffed, and that other desolate, stuffy smell.

For a time he was occupied by nothing but his pain and the choking fear of death, compared to which his pain was a relief. He could then forget his fear of death for a moment and think about the way everything had come about.

He then sensed another form of fear, a piercing, less oppressive one which he had not felt for the first time; yet now he felt it as something that had been overcome. And he clenched his fists and cursed his servants who had driven him towards death; the one into town, the old crone into the jeweller's shop, the girl into the back room, and the child by its malign counterfeit into the glass-house, from which he then saw himself stumble across horrifying stairs and bridges right under the horse's hoof. Then he fell back into great, oppressive fear. Then he whimpered like a child, not from pain but from grief and his teeth chattered.

He glared back on his life with great bitterness and denied everything that had been dear to him. He hated his untimely death so much that he hated his life since it had led him to this. This inner abandon exhausted his last strength. He felt dizzy and for a little while once more fell into a delirious, troubled sleep. Then he woke up and wanted to scream since he was still alone, but his voice failed him. Finally he vomited gall, then blood, and he died with convulsed features, his lips so contorted that his teeth and gums were bared and lent him an alien, wicked expression.

THE SOLDIER'S TALE

The dragoons of the squadron were seated on a long wooden beam that ran along the rear stable wall enjoying their midday repast. They were sitting within a narrow strip of shade cast directly on their bowed heads by the overhanging stable roof and on the zinc billycans which rested on each man's knees. A few paces away, beneath a nut tree which threw sparse flecks of black shadow over the dessicated earth, the non-commissioned officers, three platoon sergeants, the squadron bugler and a number of corporals had a bench constructed of two barrels and a board. Within the shaded strip along the wall, some kind exchange ran to and fro: it was a half audible, subdued exchange such as subordinates engage in when they feel constrained and unfree. Every now and then a repressed laugh, a cheap mumbled joke repeated by everyone ran down the line: but it did not run unbroken down the line, it had a dead spot; a sad figure at the centre upon whom the waves of harmless chatter from left to right broke. This was a person whose long, haggard face with its large ears betrayed nothing much, save that the ears jutted, were of reddish tinge and had something timorous about their inverted, folded upper rim. Like all the others, he had his bowl on his knees; but whilst with the others the zinc bottom already glinted through the fatty potato mash, his bowl was still half full. Despite this, he suddenly rose, placed his bowl on the space where he had been sitting, and departed with long, ungainly strides. Platoon sergeant Schillerwein raised his freckled, raptorial face and followed the man with his eyes. "Schwendar!" he shouted after him as the dragoon had turned the corner. A bull-necked corporal beside him threw him an enquiring glance. "I haven't liked the look of that man for some time", said the sergeant. "The fellow must be sick or something", and continued eating. Schwendar had turned the corner, had heard his name shouted behind him and had continued with bowed head along the wall which smelled of heated lime, the livid glow of the sun blazing above him, before which the transparent air hovered in immense bluish masses like dark metal turned to mist. The dragoon traversed the wide square, which divided the stables and the blinding light of the white ground, and the lime-washed wall obliterated all remoter shapes and devoured the path at his feet, so that he was suspended in a void, as it were.

Suddenly his downcast glance fell on some dark, deep water and he was shaken to the very marrow of his bones, though he was instantly aware that it was nothing more than the great vat buried in the ground from which the horses' drinking buckets were filled. But his soul had been stirred since childhood by a deep thrill in face of lightly shaded water: at home, in the corner of the little garden, between a high pile of rotting, musty leaves and a vast elderberry bush wrapped in damp, cool shade, the rain-water vat had stood in which, shortly before his birth, his mother's younger sister, a girl in the autumn of life, had drowned herself from fear of eternal damnation and hell fire. She had done this with that mysterious iron will-power given to the mentally retarded, by dowsing her head until she hung dead over the brim. To the boy this uncanny corner at twilight hours appeared to reveal the limp, slumped body of the dead woman, but this image was horribly intermingled with his own deepest life when, in hot midday hours he bent over the dark, damp mirror and his own face hovered closer out of the depths, which looked green, yet then again dissolved, swallowed up in black, twinkling circles; then a shapeless shadow seemed to thrust upwards so that he ran off with a scream and yet he returned repeatedly and stared down into it. However, that the recollection of it assailed him with such violence at that moment was but a part of that strange condition which had for weeks taken increasing possession of his mind; a kind of melancholy pensiveness which drove him into ever deeper sadness, tore his eyes open in bed and made him sense the pressure of his sluggish blood, choked his throat when he was eating and made his mind susceptible to all things alarming and sad. He knew now that he would lie down on his bed in vain; the scorching sun only made him tired, not sleepy, and inwardly he was inexplicably excited.

The recollections of his childhood were laid bare in his shattered consciousness, like corpses thrown up by an earthquake: the thrill of first Confession, of the first thunderstorm, the lurid and dull recollections of schooldays, confronted him with a child which he should address not merely as "thou" but as "I": and yet there was in him such faltering love that he no longer knew what to do with this figure; as strange to him as a strange child, in fact as incomprehensible as a dog. This sad intoxication, this inexplicable inner storm he found more troubling than the former state of depression; he preferred to try and seek diversion and entered the unfit horses' stable to see whether any new sick horses had been brought in. However he found only the three he already knew within the large, dimly lit space. The old blind grey whose colour ran to yellowish along his flanks trod the ground at his tether, weaving incessantly from right to left and again right to left.

At the neighbouring tether lay the broken-winded horse: it did not rest on tucked back legs as healthy horses do, but it lay strangely with joints half drawn back as if it constantly needed to be ready to spring up, and the head with its wide searching eyes was desperately raised up so as to draw in the air through widely distended nostrils which its chest and slack, heaving flanks so greatly needed. This was the only posture it could endure without fearing to choke to death. The rattling breathing of this horse and the dull regular beat of the weaving grey as he trod to and fro, together made up the life of this space: nothing came from the corner where the third horse stood but deathly silence. This was a large animal and it stood with its head bowed on its four legs as though asleep. But it was not asleep: while eating, it had forgotten itself, just as it could forget itself in walking and run straight ahead into a wall or into water, no less than into empty air. It was alive but life had been lost to it just as completely as to a stone that has sunk into a pond: in its dull madness it stood there neither asleep nor awake, barred from life as from death, indeed even from the possibility of dying, by some invisible, impenetrable wall: its eyes were open but they saw nothing; it knew, as it ate in its unconscious state, that from its great pendulous chaps there hung many grains of oats and amongst these lived a tiny, light-yellow maggot which squirmed and twisted in all its vitality.

When the dragoon returned across the yard he heard loud, raucous laughter drifting through the stable door. Two corporals were standing in the doorway, amusing themselves by quizzing the dragoon Moses Last about the names of the Brigadier and the Corps Commandant. This man was feeble-minded; his equestrian training had been terminated after a short spell due to insuperable coward-ice, and since he was a tailor by trade, he was put into the so-called craftsmen room; but apart from that he was assigned to general horse care and was to be seen kneeling for hours under the belly of the horses committed to his charge, lost in silent diligence as he washed their hooves with a little grey rag until they glistened like polished horn. But it was impossible to give him the least military training otherwise. If the cavalry captain, to whom he was attached in the most abject manner, dismounted at the stable door he would run out, take off his cap, and with a face distorted in joy say: "Good-day, Captain." He was not to be dissuaded from this either by the stocks or solitary confinement, neither could he be moved by any means whatsoever to remember the name of the cavalry captain or that of any other superior officer.

Schwendar gave a turn of the head in salute to the two corporals and whilst his eyes rested on them for the space of three double paces, the sight of the dunce impressed itself forcibly on him: he stood there quaking in a desperate stiff posture, his chin and neck jutting forward: from his bloated face a crooked, as it were, strained glance was directed towards his tormentors; something laboured behind his thick lips. At last a feeble ray of light lit up his face; he squeezed out some words and in his zeal thrust himself close to the corporal and with a loose gesture seized him by the buttons of his uniform. The corporal then roared some kind of command and Schwendar just saw the bloated face jerk back before the clenched fist drawn back before delivering its blow. He walked on with rapid strides up to the privates' room, and since it was Sunday put on his walking-out uniform; then he took up helmet and sabre to go into town. Once ready he searched for his old silver watch out of habit and at once remembered he no longer possessed it; he realized that he had groped for it daily for the past two months and had come to the same sense of humiliation and dull pain on remembering the circumstances of its loss. The thief was his only friend. It was the squadron harness maker Thoma, now confined to Spielberg gaol.

...

He plunged on ever deeper into the forest. He trudged on between the birch trees like a drunken man, his sabre trailing behind and his helmet shoved back on the nape of his neck. The low branches struck his heated face, his feet left deep traces in the boggy ground which filled gurgling with brownish black water. The sound brought the thought of death as close to him as had the sight of the water bucket earlier in the day, and in order to cease hearing it he changed direction and ran rather than walked through a clearing which offered firmer ground. Ahead the forest appeared to thin out. A reddish hue hovered before his eyes; a reddish blue shimmer of light fell across the path. As he drew nearer there were numerous sage blossoms between the dusky bushes. He looked fixedly at them but as he raised his eyes and walked on, the reddish hue drifted off before him once more like a hovering veil. Then it lay across the stem of a low-bending birch which leaned sideways furtively and half-hidden, like a red patch. Then it encroached from all sides, an entire blood-red veil, and cast great bloody patches over the rounded greenery of dense bushes and over the white stems. Pools of blood were there, stretching across the darkening earth. Ten leaps, to each of which his pounding heart seemed to deny all strength, brought him to the edge of the forest. Bathed in blood, suffused by a motionless, overly intense gleam as though illumined by the final glance of eyes breaking in death, the endless, undulating plain lay before him. Behind the great railway embankment, which lay two hours' ride away, the sun was setting. No more than the uppermost rim of the naked, glowing disc blinked over the dam like the uppermost part of an eye exposed by the eyelids: then this last sparkling remnant fell down and slowly the glow of the landscape sank into its abyss, its death, out of which the red mist drifted skywards. Exhausted by fear and running, Schwendar had sat down by the edge of the forest. As he removed his heavy helmet and placed it in the grass beside him, he felt as if a cold, keen and yet indifferent glance was directed his way from the bushes to the side, and he felt his breast stifled by a feeling that had to be connected with some remote memory. It was the memory of the day on which his mother had died, a dull, bodily memory rather than of the soul. He felt a choking of his breath and a chill at his back when the sick woman suddenly sat up and said with a strange, hard and strong voice: "It's the holy Virgin Mary, she's waving to me with a light, and again, she's waving to me with a light." Then the dying woman's glances passed slowly, with a look of severity and utter detachment over the young boy, over him and over all that remained in the room; finally over the raised part of the blanket where her own thin feet lay, and finally came to rest, rigid and full of acute, strained attention, as though directed inwards; while horror silently bored its way into the boy's soul at this horrific idea that a figure he could not see was calling his mother to follow her and that she was so greatly in thrall to this strange woman that her open eyes saw nothing else; not him nor anything else in the world. All these things were aroused in him and brought with them a bitterness from which there was no possible escape. Once again he experienced that inner petrified state of the child at the insight that such a thing could happen; but now, since it had already happened so long ago, he saw it in a new and terrible light: he hated his mother for having stolen away out of life like that, with a cold, empty glance at him and at everything she was leaving behind in this hell. He felt the lawn on which he was sitting to be part of that great impenetrable covering under which the dead had crept so as to get away from it all. They lay beneath it like sleepers who wrap themselves in their stuffy feather-beds and bury their face in pillows; and their ears were full of earth so that they could not hear his groans and paid no heed to his desolation. He jumped up and struck the ground with his feet so that his spurs left deep cuts in the earth and the wispy strips of lawn flew up high. Then he drew his sabre and began in senseless rage to slash at the bushes and little trees, intoxicated by the sensation of being a destroyer. He believed that he could sense feeble resistance and the indignant breath of those who were subdued by him. Shredded foliage filled the air and the sap from wounded branches was sprayed over the soldier's face and hands. The sabre slashed gaping clefts into the cool darkness which welled up towards him as though out of deep cellars. He sprang back, for now he was touched by a rigid, deathly glance at close quarters; at his feet some wretched being appeared to be cowering in the gloom. His sabre swept down on some soft body, and having flung it aside, saw it was the pitiful little corpse of a dead hare whose stark eyes now looked with lifeless stare into the depths of the high, cool sky. This piteous sight increased the miserable man's dull rage; once more he dashed towards the dead animal and flung it aside in a great arc so that it struck with a slap against a hard tree trunk and instantly drove a flock of startled jackdaws high above fleeing into the still air with revolting cries and a flurry of wings. Their cries drew the soldier's eyes upwards. The ugly flock took wing from the topmost branches of a gigantic elm which seemed to toy with the burden of a green citadel built high upon a steep slope and resting on ancient roots. But to the side of the elm there rose two giant poplars and thrust their towering tops high into the twilit sky. The two trees were not intertwined but their boundless, mighty striving seemed to relate one to the other: the threefold aspiring might of the elm captured the height-seeking gaze as though lifted by powerful arms; a living, shadow-filled bower guided it aloft to the next, until the last then transferred it to the poplars; these reared up together in silence as though enthralled by inner flames of soundless emulation. The sight of the three trees ever increasing to gigantic stature in the growing gloom weighed like a nightmare on Schwander; the thought of striking at these unshakable trunks with his sabre made his arm heavy like a lame limb. The might of these secret giant powers robbed his senseless sport of all heady sense of superiority that might momentarily have triumphed over his sense of weakness or fear; it calmed his blood and once more thrust him into a void. He took his helmet up from the ground and ran off, straight across the open pasture towards the barracks, his bared sabre in one hand, his helmet in the other. He had only one thought; to be no longer alone: his fear had acquired preciseness; he felt as if the burden with which these giant trees were toying would now be cast upon his soul. He had already run for some distance when he perceived amidst the throbbing of his arteries the furious, rapid hoof-beats of a horse which must be chasing him and with every dull reverberation was gaining another span of the intervening ground. Without further thought he flung himself sideways like a hunted hare and stormed towards the forest with great strides. At the point where the sluice of the manorial fish pond adjoins the forest, he leaped across the dry drainage ditch and ran along the pond, scaring the great dark fish by his unruly shadow, like some deranged sacristan figure, so that they shot apart in a circle as though struck by a flung stone and vanished into the greenish black, dank, hidden depths. The young officer who had galloped after him out of curiosity reined in his great panting chestnut mount and followed the inscrutable figure with his eyes as it fled through the trees, leaping like a savage and desperately brandishing its helmet and sabre with long arms.

...

He straightened up. Bright moonlight was shed over the two long rows of uniform beds and strong dark shadows separated the sleeping bodies like deep chasms. The dark patches under their eyes and lips gave their faces a strange enlarged appearance. Schwander had sat up. His hands, whose weight he felt as if they were dead, lay stretched out before him on the blanket. His eyes travelled across the sleepers with a restless and empty expression. Being awake was no better than lying half asleep with closed eyes. It seemed as if the stone that had lain upon his chest were hovering at some distance before him, somewhere to the right in the area around the dusky corner where the troupe's bugle was suspended; it seemed to hover there motionless in the twilight, and from there alarmed his breast with the same paralysing burden as before. He turned his head to one side so as not to see it and exerted all his strength to force his thoughts onto that which lay before him. It struck him as possible that with superhuman exertion one could force one's thoughts outwards so that they would have to turn their backs on what oppressed him within. The man lying nearest to him was corporal Taborsky. He was a cobbler in civilian life. He lay on his back as stiff as a ramrod. He had also stretched out his arms straight to right and left. He was a genial person who had some regard for good manners. His little straw-yellow moustache jutted out under his pug nose from his contented looking face and stirred with every calm breath he took. In this, as it were, benevolent regularity of his breathing also lay an expression of that which distinguished him in his service. No one looked on a horse at his fodder with such benevolence, no one listened to swearing and complaint with so friendly, detached a face. He could walk up and down in the stable for hours, always casting a friendly glance into each mirror fragment that had been fixed to the wooden posts for adjusting one's neckerchief, then to nod calmly yet with a trace of irony and pass on again. Beneath his pillow lay a folded handkerchief which he never used and a few pages of a trashy novel. He rather relished reading some of these with a certain degree of ostentation, but preferred even more to be asked why he so much enjoyed reading and to render account on this; and in general to speak about the distinction between educated people and those who resembled dumb animals. All at once, in an instant, Schwendar knew that all thoughts had reached their conclusion and that all he was capable of thinking about this man had been thought through; and that it would be quite as pointless to look at him any longer as it would be for a thirsty man to possess a jug which contained no drop of water. And he began to sense within him the resurgence of a fear relentlessly approaching from afar which would relentlessly wash away this wretched dam constructed of sand – this thinking about the man lying next to him – if he did not quickly fortify it. Yet he scarcely had the courage to divert his glance from the corporal towards the adjacent bed, for in doing so it would have to pass over the dark space between these two beds; and within this abyss filled with shadow he felt there lay the confirmation of horror, the unavoidable reality and the ludicrous futility of any semblance of escape. Like a cowardly thief who between two intakes of breath lifts his foot over the sleeper, so engrossed in his own heart-beat that the ground seems quite distant and the power to control his feet infinitely little. He raised his glance stealthily and trembling across the dark strip, with utmost control and almost caressingly let it glide over the face of the next man, who rested both arms under his head and slept open-mouthed, so that you could see his strong fine teeth and the nostrils of his upturned nose. This was the dragoon Cypris, a childish person whose brown cheeks showed dimples when he laughed. And he greatly loved to laugh. Schwendar tried to remind himself of the sound of his quiet, inexhaustible laughter: it was like the high-toned gurgle in the neck of a glass bottle. This man Cypris was wrapped up in his blanket like a child. Opposite him, in the other row of beds lay the powerful Nekolar. He was twenty years old but of vast stature and the strongest man in the squadron. His hair was fine and short and thickly grown like an otter's fur and had a colour of gleaming brightness. He lay with his face buried in the pillow and his great limbs were flung across the bed as if it was some big, dull coloured animal with which he wrestled and had pressed to earth with the muscular power of his young, mighty body. Schwendar averted his glance from him with gloomy amazement and perused his neighbour. This man was called Karasek. His face was ugly and mean and he lay in his bed in ugly posture, the blanket pulled up to his fat chin, his knees drawn up, at once cowardly and disreputable. Schwendar withdrew his glance from him in sadness and disgust and remained on the empty resting place of his friend Thoma the harness-maker who was confined to the guard-room. Here he was overwhelmed by a sense of desolation: his friend had betrayed and bartered him, his mother had sunk beneath the earth, his throat was choked up against food, his limbs could no longer carry him, and sleep repelled him. Benumbed he propped himself on one arm then on the other. Then, in a feverish impulse, rather to change his position than from any inner motive, he threw off the blanket and knelt down on his bed. My God, my God, my God, he moaned half aloud to himself and rolled his eyes like a suffering animal. The room grew ever brighter, the proximity of these men oppressed him more and more as they lay there wrapped in their sleeping bodies and paid no heed to his torments. A dim recollection put the words in his mouth. "My God, my Lord, let this cup pass from me!" He repeated them three or four times, until suddenly something inexplicable came about. Within the light, which filled the whole room with its brightness, a change took place. It lasted only for a moment; it seemed to come from within but may have come from outside. It was no more than a brief flash, like the signal from a distant light. Then the silent light sank away into itself again and everything was as before. But with supernatural speed a presentiment took possession of his soul, the certainty that it had been a sign to him: the reflexion of the open heavens, the gleam of an angel gliding through the house. With open mouth and loosened limbs he turned on his knees towards the window.

The blue-black sky gleaming in tremendous silence receded at his gaze and appeared to know of nothing. However the soft light of the low-lying moon lay upon the earth, embraced the smithy and the red-tiled house where the NCO's lived with an unaccustomed gleam, made the barriers of the open riding schools appear slimmer, rounded the sharp edges of the newly-dug trenches and welded the ploughed fields and great drill square into a single broad landscape overcast by an airy gleam; the vast gloomy dam on the furthest horizon caught the eye only to steer it away like some huge raised unswerving pathway leading to the unknown. Yet Schwendar's eyes, which began to fill with a damp gleam, sought something within this whole great realm that might be smaller, like the quickening glance of the human eye, and yet large enough for it to flow through the space between heaven and earth and render all human dimensions void. His eyes sought the place from which the sign had originated, for he knew that it had been a sign and that it was meant for him. Faith had leaped back into his empty soul with one great silent impulse and now pervaded him like a gentle, silent tide borne on by a mysterious mellowness. No longer a mere void inwardly hollowed out by emptiness and sorrow, by fruitless groaning; but now transformed, dimly aware of an inalienable joy, he knelt down with his white shirt and his heavy eyes, with lips open in yearning over the bodies of those who slept, as they lay buried deep in their stuffy beds, gnashing their teeth against the darkness. Yet he wished to savour once more the ineffable joy of this beginning, which seemed to him more desirable than the minutes that had passed since; to feel once again the gentle breath, the soundless dawning with which something immense had been bestowed on him throughout that silent night, and beneath whose gentle passing the moon's brightness had silently increased, then waned and faded away. However, as to the repetition of the sign failing and everything then collapsing into nothingness; to prevent this, he formed the idea of having a wish with an inner reservation scarcely apparent to himself: he permitted the Lord in advance to hold back his second sign, and this too should signify nothing evil. His face took on a cunning and fearful expression: he became conscious of the sound made by his breathing and stopped short. At that moment the conviction overcame him that something had occurred in a part of the heavens, which his eyes could not survey. He could not tell what it was, yet it had come to pass. An inner force drew him closer to the window and bent his glance towards that side of the horizon, which now emerged. It was there: just where an elm tree, jammed between two giant poplars, lifted its ghostly canopy of branches against the dark, impenetrable sky; there It was, half motion, half incandescence, it lay between the tree-tops as though an angel's heel had in descent brushed the swaying black baldachin, imperceptibly, as if a little bird had lifted its wing in the high bright air, and yet it was movement of a stupendous kind; as if many squadrons had mustered upon great pastures behind distant little clouds of dust, whose approach made the earth reverberate in perceptible waves like subterranean thunder.

After the sign had been repeated, Schwendar let himself slip down and pressed his forehead against the foot of the bed with a feeling of innermost joy. He felt as light as a new-born child: all heaviness, all torments seemed to drain away into the distance, like the burbling of brooks from deepest valleys for someone who is raised up upon the summit of an immense mountain.

He put on his stable clogs and denims, and then sat down on his bed and waited with an easy heart until he heard the heavy tread of the duty corporal on the stairs, who was on his way to relieve the stable guards. He then rose and entered the stable. He was met on the stairs by three or four men being relieved and who were going to bed. Their dull, morose faces and their haste to crawl into bed aroused genial astonishment in him, such as the antics of children might in an adult. At the stable door, where it was dark, a drunken sergeant who imagined he was the duty officer and had to order matters, collided with him so violently that he tottered into the little gutter that runs around every stable; but the sense of inward joy which filled him only increased with every physical contact and spontaneous joyfulness sprang from his heart's core, which turned into a smile on his face as with someone deeply in love; to a smile which arose ever and again like airy bubbles at the end of a water spout. All things fed his cheerfulness: the hurried racing about between stables, which always occurred at the point of relief, the cursing of the drunken sergeant which died away in the distance. When a dragoon who belonged to another unit came running barefoot into his stable by mistake, to fetch his missing stable-clogs, he had to laugh out aloud and said inwardly to himself: "things are running wild like at a wedding." Wholly at ease, he walked up and down between the silent horses in the semi-dark stable where they lay or stood asleep, with easy, swaggering strides like a rich farmer, only that he did not have hands held behind his back, but in front.

THE VILLAGE IN THE MOUNTAINS

I

In June it was the townspeople who arrived and they take up all the large rooms. The farmers and their womenfolk sleep in the attics hung full of horses' tackle, full of dusty sleigh trappings fitted with their jingling little yellow bells, old heavy winter jackets, old flint-lock guns and bulky rust-covered saws. They have removed all their belongings from the lower rooms and emptied all chests for the townspeople and nothing in the rooms remains but the scent of the cellar mixed with great cream vats and old wood, which drifts out through the little windows from the interior of the house and hovers in invisible columns, somewhat sour and cool, over the heads of the pale red mallows, as far as the tall apple trees.

Only the wall decorations have been left: the antlers and the many little images of the Virgin Mary and the saints in carved and cardboard frames, between which there hang rosaries made of artificial corals or tiny wooden beads. The townswomen hang their large garden hats and coloured parasols on the antlers; into the loop of a rosary, they fasten the picture of an actress whose regal shoulders and raised eyebrows express some great pain with inimitable charm; the pictures of young men, of famous older people and of women with unnatural smiles they prop up against the back of a little wax lamb bearing the banner of the Cross, or they pin them between the wall and a gilded heart within whose scarlet wounds seven little swords are thrust.

Yet they themselves, the women and girls from town, are to be seen sitting everywhere in places no one else ever sits: at both ends of the wooden pails of a well, where the water sprayed back by the wind is blown into their hair, until this is filled with dew like fine, close-spun spider-web in the morning. Or they sit on the stile where they prove an obstacle to everyone whose path lies that way. But they know nothing of the fact that someone has to pass just that way, just to that particular field between the two fences and the deeply carved, gushing brook. For them it is all the same where one goes. There lies something so random, so effortless in their existence. They have no need of a day of rest and can make of any hour what they choose. So it is with their singing. They do not sing in church and not to accompany a dance. Suddenly, at evening, when it grows dark and shafts of light beam from many little windows between the sombre trees and across paths, they start to sing, one here and one there. Their songs seem to be a mixture of multiple tones, at times quite akin to a dancing song, at times to a church hymn: it contains a lightness and sovereignty over life. When they cease the darkening valley resume its sluggish life once again: one hears the gushing sound of the great brook, welling up and then dying away, and here and there the isolated gushing of a little wooden channelled well. Or the orchard trees shake themselves and send a shower of rustling drops fall from above through all their branches – as suddenly as the brief unexpected sigh of a sleeper – and this startles the hedgehog who hurries on his way.

A few of the shafts of light do not extinguish for a long while and are still there when the Plough has slipped down to the rim of the sky and its lowest stare rest on the mountain ridge and shimmer unsteadily through the tops of the giant larches. Those are the rooms in which a young girl gleans from a book the possibilities of life and breathes bewildered as though touched by music which both intoxicates and subdues; or those in which a woman of riper years, in her fearful and astounded thoughts, cannot master the notion that this dreamlike Here and Now for her signifies the Inescapable, the Real. From these windows candlelight is constantly shed, piercing through the apple trees, it throws a beam across the meadow and the stone dam, right down to the black surface of the lake which seems to fling it back and carry it like a pale yellow shimmer poured forth. Yet it also dips down and casts a plangent shaft into the moist darkness where the black-grey perch rest in dull stasis and the restless little white fish ceaselessly quiver like quaking grass.

II

On the lawns they map out their square tennis-courts and fence them in with high grey nets. From a distance they resemble monstrous cobwebs. Whoever stands indoors sees the landscape as though painted on Japanese jugs where the enamel is permeated by regular, fine fissures: the blue-green lake, the white shore-line, the forest of firs, the rocks above it and at the zenith a sky of delicate hue like pale heather blossom; all of this sustains the fine grey squares of netting.

On the undulating hills that lie to the far side of the road, they are ploughing. Whenever the players change ends so as to fairly distribute sun and wind, then the ploughmen turn their heavy teams about and with a powerful heave thrust the plough-shear into the start of a new furrow. The ploughmen plough evenly; like a weighty vessel the plough furrows its way through the rich soil, and those great hands tanned by the air and labour, rest with heavy pressure upon the haft. The game played by the four players alternates. At times one is dominant. The entire game is contained by his strokes which are calm and full like the paw-strokes of a young lion. The flying balls and the other players, indeed the grass surface and the nets in which the image of forests and clouds is captured, everything follows his wrist, mysteriously held fast as if by a powerful magnet.

Another player is weak, quite weak. Between him and each of his strokes thinking intrudes. He has to look on at himself. His movements consist of profound untruth:

at times they are the movements of a fencer with a foil and at others the movements of one who tries to fend off stones.

A third is indifferent about the game. He senses a woman's glance on him, on his hands, on his cheeks, on his temples. At times he closes his eyes so as to feel it on his eyelids. He lives in the evening that has passed: for this woman, whose glance he senses on him, is not present. Sometimes he runs quite distracted for a few paces to where no ball has dropped. Just the same, he does not play quite so badly. At times he hits with great, relaxed motion like someone emerging from sleep clutching the air after fruit he dreamt of. And the ball he touches then flies back with even greater force than any stroke by the strong player. It bores itself into the lawn and no longer bounces back.

The game for the four players alternates: tomorrow, perhaps, the indifferent man will take the place of the strong one. Perhaps vain and bold recollections and the intake of the morning air will make him into the strongest who today was quite feeble.

But the ploughmen plough evenly and the dark furrows run straight through the heavy soil.

CAVALRY TALE

Before six a.m. on the 22nd of July 1848 the second squadron, a detachment of Wallmoden cuirassiers led by Cavalry Captain Baron Rofrano, left the casino San Allesandro with a hundred and seven horsemen and rode in the direction of Milan. An indescribable silence lay over the open, radiant landscape; morning clouds climbed the gleaming sky from the heights of the distant mountains like silent billows of smoke; the maize stood motionless and between clumps of trees that looked almost washed there gleamed country houses and churches. Scarcely had the detachment left behind it the last outposts of its own army by about a mile, than weapons suddenly glinted amongst the corn fields and the avant-garde reported enemy infantry. The squadron formed up along the highway for attack but was met with a flurry of singularly loud, almost mewing volleys of shot; it attacked straight across the field and drove a troop of irregularly armed men before it like quails. These were men of the Manaras Legion wearing their strange headgear. The prisoners were handed over to a corporal and eight privates and sent to the rear. The avant-garde reported suspicious figures in front of a lovely villa whose entrance avenue was flanked by ancient cypress trees. Sergeant Anton Lerch dismounted, took twelve men armed with carbines, surrounded the windows and took eighteen students of the Pisa Legion prisoner; well-bred and handsome young men with white hands and shoulder-length hair. Half an hour later the squadron seized a man passing by who was dressed in Bergamo attire and came under suspicion through his all too harmless and inconspicuous demeanour. This man carried, sewn into the lining of his jacket, the most important detailed plans on the establishment of volunteer corps in the Guidicari region and their liaison with the Piedmontese army. At around ten o'clock in the morning a herd of cattle fell into the hands of the reconnaissance troop. Immediately after this a relatively strong force confronted them and opened fire on the avant-garde from behind a cemetery wall. Lieutenant Graf Trautsohn's advance column leaped the low wall and fell upon the totally confounded enemy amongst the graves, a great number of whom sought refuge in the church and from there escaped through the sacristy into some dense woodland. The twenty-seven new captives declared themselves to be Neapolitan volunteers under papal officers. The squadron counted one dead. A platoon riding around the copse, consisting of Corporal Wotrubek and the dragoons Holl and Haindl, captured a light howitzer drawn by two plough-horses, by falling upon the escort, seizing the horses by their halter and turning them back. Corporal Wotrubek, being lightly wounded, was sent back to headquarters with a report on the successful engagements and other fortunate events, the prisoners were also transported to the rear, but the howitzer taken along by the remaining eighty-seven strong squadron of horses after the escort had been withdrawn.

After the city of Milan had been totally evacuated of all enemy troops, both regular and irregular according to congruent reports by various prisoners, and also emptied of all artillery and military supplies, the Cavalry Captain could hardly deny himself and his squadron the pleasure of riding into this great, beautiful city lying defenceless before him. Amidst the pealing of noonday bells, the rallying march resounded from four bugles into the steely, sparkling sky, reverberating from a thousand windows and flashed back upon seventy-eight cuirassiers, seventy-eight uplifted naked blades; streets to right and left were filled with astounded faces like an anthill stirred to life; cursing wan figures fleeing behind the gateways of houses, drowsy windows flung open by the naked arms of unknown beauties; past Santo Babila, San Fidele, San Carlo, past the world-renowned marble cathedral, past San Satiro, San Giorgio, San Lorenzo, San Eustorgio whose ancient bronze gates all opened and where silver saints and bright-eyed, brocaded women beckoned from candle-light and incense fumes; ever alert to shots from a thousand attic rooms, dusky gateways, low boutiques; and then ever again mere half-grown girls and boys displaying their white teeth and dark hair; looking down on all this from a trotting horse with sparkling eyes through a mask of blood-speckled dust: that is how the fine squadron rode through Milan.

Not far from the last-named gateway where a glacis overgrown with lovely plane trees stretched out, Sergeant Anton Lech thought he saw the familiar face of a woman at the ground-floor window of a newly-built, bright yellow house. Curiosity prompted him to turn about in his saddle, and judging also from certain stiff strides taken by his horse that a stone in the road had pierced one of its front hooves, he rode to the rear of the squadron and could exit without disrupting formation; all this prompted him to dismount at the very moment he had steered his horse into the entrance of the house concerned. Scarcely had he lifted the second white-clad foreleg of his bay so as to examine the hoof, when an interior door giving onto the hallway did indeed open and a buxom, youngish woman in somewhat dishevelled morning attire appeared, whilst behind her a brightly lit room with green garden-facing windows where a few pots of basil and red geraniums could be seen by the sergeant; in addition there was a mahogany cupboard and a mythological biscuit ware group, while his sharp glance simultaneously caught a glimpse of the opposite wall of the room in a pier glass, filled by a large bed and a concealed door through which a stout, well-shaven, mature man at that instant withdrew.

Yet meanwhile the woman's name was called to mind by the sergeant and a host of other things besides: that she was the widow or divorced wife of a Croatian NCO bookkeeper, that some nine or ten years past in Vienna he had spent several evenings and half nights in the company of another of her former lovers of the day; so he now tried with his eyes to recall the former sumptuous, slender figure beneath her present fullness. However, the woman standing there smiled at him in a half flattered, Slavic way which drove the blood into his powerful neck and under his eyes, whilst a certain mannered affectation with which she addressed him, no less than her morning attire and the room furnishings, intimidated him. Yet at the very moment that his languid glance followed a large fly that ran over the woman's hair-comb and outwardly heeded nothing but how he, in whisking this fly away, should then lay his hand upon her white, warm, fresh neck, the consciousness of the skirmishes won that day and other lucky events filled him so completely that he pressed her head forward with a heavy hand as he said: "Vuic" – her baptismal name – "in eight days we're entering the town and then this here will be my quarters," pointing to the half-open door of the room. Meanwhile he heard several doors in the house slam shut, felt himself urged on by his horse, first by dumb tugging at the reins, then by its loud whinnying response to others; he mounted and trotted off after the squadron, his head ducked, without taking with him any response from Vuic other than an embarrassed laugh. But the word once uttered established his power of authority. Riding at a pace that was no longer brisk, separate from the mounted column, beneath the heavy metallic glare of the sky, his glance caught up in the accompanying cloud of dust, the sergeant's thoughts dwelt ever more within the room with the mahogany furniture and the pots of basil, and also within a civilian atmosphere still permeated by the element of war, an atmosphere of comfortable living and congenial violence, without service commitment, a slippered existence, with the sabre-guard thrust through the left pocket of a dressing-gown. The clean-shaven, portly man who had vanished through the hidden door, a being something between a clergyman and a retired chamberlain, played a significant part in this, almost greater than the splendid wide bed and Vuic's delicate white skin. The shaven man assumed the position now of a confidentially treated, somewhat grovelling friend who had trafficked court gossip, fetched tobacco and capons, now was pressed to the wall, was forced to pay hush money, had ties with all manner of intrigues, was a Piedmont confidant, papal cook, procurer, owner of suspicious houses with dark arbours for political conspiracy, and grew into a gigantic flabby figure into whose body one might punch plug-holes in twenty places to extract gold instead of blood.

The patrol encountered nothing new during the afternoon hours and the sergeant's reveries knew no inhi-bitions. But in him was aroused a thirst for unexpected gain, for bonuses, for ducats suddenly filling his pockets. For the thought of that first future entry into the room with the mahogany furniture was the splinter in his flesh around which all wishes and desires festered.

Now as the reconnaissance detachment, their horses fed and partly rested, set off to advance in an arc towards Lodi and the bridge at Adda (where contact with the enemy was clearly to be expected) the sergeant found a village at some remove from the highway, with a half ruined steeple and secluded in a shadowy hollow, suspect in some enticing way; so in summoning the privates Holl and Scarmolin, he turned aside with both of these from the squadron's route, hoping to surprise nothing less than an enemy general under scant protection, to attack or otherwise gain some extraordinary premium; that was how much his imagination was aroused. Having reached this miserable, seemingly deserted little nest, he ordered Scarmolin to ride round the outlying houses to the left, Holl the houses to the right, whilst he himself with pistol at the ready prepared to gallop through the street; but soon, as he felt hard stone flags underfoot over which, furthermore, some kind of slippery fat had been spilled, he had to slow down his horse to a walk. The village remained deathly quiet; no child, no bird, not a breath of air. To right and left there stood dirty little dwellings with walls that has lost their mortar; here and there something ugly had been drawn in charcoal upon the naked bricks; peering through stripped doorposts into the interior, here and there the sergeant saw some foul, naked figure lounging on a bedstead or dragging itself with dislocated hips through the room. His horse trod heavily, laboriously pushing its hind legs forward as though they were made of lead. As he turned around and bent to check the rear horseshoe, slurred footsteps came from a house and as he straightened up, some wench whose face he could not see passed close by his horse. She was only half dressed; her dirty, tattered skirt of flowered silk dragged along the gutter, her naked feet tucked into dirty slippers; she passed so close to the horse that the breath from its nostrils stirred the greasy, shiny bundle of curls which hung down her exposed neck from under an old straw hat; and yet she did not quicken her step or evade the horseman. To the left beneath a threshold two bleeding, embattled rats rolled out into the middle of the street one of which screeched so piteously in defeat that the sergeant's horse stopped and stared at the ground with head askew, breathing audibly. A squeeze of the thighs urged it on once more; and now the woman had vanished in a hallway without the sergeant having been able to see her face. From the next house a dog busily ran out with its head raised, dropped a bone in the middle of the street and tried to bury it in a crack of the paving. It was a white, unclean bitch with dangling tits; she burrowed away with fiendish zeal, then caught the bone up in her teeth and carried it a little further. While she resumed her burrowing three other dogs joined her: two were very young, with soft bones and flabby skin; without barking and unable to bite they tugged one another by the lips with blunt teeth. The dog which had also joined them was a light-yellow whippet with so swollen a belly that it could only drag itself along slowly on its four skinny legs. Perched on that fat body which was taut as a drum, the head appeared far too small; in its little restless eyes there lurked a horrific expression of pain and oppression. All at once two more dogs sprang to join them: one was haggard, white and of extreme, voracious ugliness, from whose enflamed eyes black streaks oozed down, and a miserable dachshund on lanky legs. The latter raised his head towards the sergeant and gazed at him. He must have been very old. His eyes were infinitely weary and sad. The bitch, however, ran to and fro in stupid haste before the horseman; the two young ones snapped silently at the horse's ankles with their soft jaws and the whippet dragged its horrid body right in front of its hooves. The brown mount could not move another step. But when the sergeant thought to fire his pistol at one of the animals, he gave his horse both spurs and sped resonantly over the paving. Yet after a few spurts he had to rein in his horse hard. For his path was now blocked by a cow dragged along by a young lad on a taut rope to the slaughter house. But the cow, recoiling from the vapour of blood and the fresh hide of a black calf nailed to the door-post, dug its feet in, sucked in the ruddy haze of sunset through bulging nostrils before the young lad could subdue her by his blows and the rope and then with pitiful eyes tore off a last mouthful of hay which the sergeant had tied to the front of his saddle. He had now passed the last house in the village and riding between two low, crumbling walls beyond an ancient single-arched stone bridge over an apparently dry ditch, he could survey the course of the path ahead, yet felt in his horse's gait such indescribable heaviness, such a sense of not advancing, that every foot along the walls to left and right, indeed every millipede and woodlouse perched there, passed laboriously before his glance as though he had squandered an immeasurable span of time in riding through this revolting village. But now that heavy, raucous breathing rose from his horse's chest and he did not at once correctly identify this unwonted sound, first seeking its cause either above or beside him and finally in the distance, he noticed beyond the stone bridge (and incidentally the same distance away as himself) a horseman from his own regiment approaching; indeed, it was a sergeant mounted on a chestnut with white-shod front legs. Since he well knew that such a horse did not exist within the entire squadron apart from the one which he himself rode at that very moment, and since he was as yet unable to recognize the other horse-man's face, he even spurred on his horse impatiently to a brisk trot, whereupon the other man also quickened his pace in the very same measure. Yet now they were sepa-rated by no more than a stone's throw and whilst the two horses, each from its side, stepped up to the bridge with the same white-shod front leg, – the sergeant with fixed stare recognizing himself in the apparition – he pulled back his horse in desperation and stretched out his right hand with outspread fingers towards this being; where-upon the figure, equally parrying and raising its right hand suddenly vanished. The privates Holl and Scarmolin appeared to the right and left with unperturbed expres-sions on their faces from the dry ditch while at the same time the squadron's bugles sounded the charge from quite close by. Climbing a rise at the fiercest gallop the sergeant could already see the squadron galloping towards a copse out of which enemy cavalry with pikes were keenly storming out; as he gathered all four loose reins in his left hand and wound the strap about his right, he saw how the fourth column split off from the squadron and slackened pace; he rode now on resonant ground, now in strong dusty odour, now in the thick of the enemy; he slashed at a blue arm that carried a pike, glimpsed close by the captain's face wide-eyed with teeth grimly bared; next was wedged between numerous enemy faces and foreign colours, was swallowed up by numerous bran-dished sabres; thrust the closest man through the neck and off his horse; saw private Scarmolin close by with laughing face; cut through the fingers of a bridle-hand

and deep into the horse's neck; felt the mêlée loosening and was suddenly alone by the banks of a little brook, behind an enemy officer on an iron-grey horse. The officer was trying to cross the brook; the iron-grey refused. The officer swiftly reined him about and turned a youthful, very pale face and the muzzle of a pistol towards the sergeant, when a sabre was driven through his mouth with the full might of a galloping horse gathered into its little tip. The sergeant drew back his sabre and at the very spot where the fingers of the falling man had released his mount, snatched up the reins of the iron-grey as it lifted its feet over its dying master with the delicacy of a doe.

As the sergeant rode back with the beautiful mount as booty, the sun as it set in its heavy mist cast a flood of redness over the pastureland. Even where there were no hoof-prints entire pools of blood appeared to lie. A red reflection fell upon the white uniforms and the laughing faces, the cuirasses and caparisons sparkled and glowed, and most strongly of all, on three little fig-trees whose soft leaves the laughing horsemen had used to wipe the blood-channels of their sabres. The sergeant halted to the side of the red-flecked trees and beside him the squadron bugler raised a bugle, which seemed bathed in red juice, to his mouth and sounded the fall-in. The sergeant rode from one column to the next and noted that the squadron had not lost a man, and instead had captured nine led horses. He rode over to the cavalry captain and made his report, his iron-grey ever at his side, which pranced along with its head held high and drew in the air like the young, beautiful and proud horse that it was. The captain only listened distractedly to the report. He gestured to Lieutenant Count Trautsohn to come over to him, who immediately dismounted and at once uncoupled the light howitzer captured behind the lines with six dismounted cuirassiers, and had the gun hauled away by the six teams and sunk in a small marshy pool formed by the brook. Thereupon he remounted, and having chased off with a flat blade the two now superfluous draught-horses, silently took his place once more at the head of the first column. Meanwhile the squadron which had formed up in two sections had not actually been restive, yet there existed something of an unusual mood, to be explained by the excitement of four successful engagements in one day, and now expressed in little bursts of half-suppressed laughter as well as the exchange of subdued calls. The horses too did not stand still, especially among those where strange captured horses had been introduced. After such good fortunes the muster space seemed too restrictive to all of them and these horsemen and victors inwardly desired to launch out against a new adversary in open formation, to lay at him and capture new mounts. At that moment Captain of Cavalry Baron Rofrano rode close along the front of his squadron and raising his heavy eyelids from his somewhat sleepy blue eyes, he gave the clear command without raising his voice: "Release all off-horses!" The squadron stood in deathly calm. Only the iron-grey beside the sergeant almost touched the forehead of the horse on which the captain was seated with its nostrils. The captain sheathed his sabre, drew one of his pistols from its holster and in wiping a little dust off the gleaming barrel with the back of his bridle-hand, he repeated his command in a slightly louder voice and immediately after counted "one" and "two". Having counted "two" he turned his veiled glance towards the sergeant sitting before him in the saddle who stared fixedly back at him. Whilst Anton Lerch's enduring fixed glance may have expressed a certain degree of devoted trust resulting from many years' commitment to service, his consciousness was almost oblivious of the tremendous suspense of this moment but rather swamped by numerous images of a weird sense of well-being; and out of innermost depths quite unknown to himself there arose such ferocious rage against the person before him who wished to deprive him of his horse, which affected his face, voice and demeanour, indeed the man's entire being, such as can only arise in mysterious fashion through many years of close communal living. But whether something similar was taking place in the Captain or whether at this moment of dumb insubordination the whole silent, enveloping menace of critical situations seemed to come to a head, remains open to doubt. As he lifted his arm with a nonchalant, almost affected movement, and curling his upper lip disdainfully counted "three", the shot already rang out and the sergeant, struck in the forehead, sank down on the neck of his horse and then fell to earth between the chestnut and the iron-grey. Yet scarcely had he hit the ground, before all other ranks and privates rid themselves of their captured mounts with a tug at the reins or a kick. The Captain, calmly returning his pistol to its holster, was then able to lead off the squadron, still reeling from such a lightening-blow, against an enemy that was apparently rallying once more in the hazy, nebulous distance. The enemy, however, did not respond to the renewed attack and shortly afterwards the reconnaissance detachment arrived unscathed at the southern post of its own army.

THE EXPERIENCE OF MARSHALL BASSOMPIERRE

At a certain time in my life my service commitments involved me in crossing a small bridge quite regularly several times a week at a given hour (since the Pont Neuf had not as yet been built) and in being recognized and greeted mostly by labourers or other members of the community, yet most conspicuously and regularly by a very pretty tradeswoman whose shop was marked by a sign with two angels; and whenever I passed during those five or six months, would bow low and follow me with her eyes as long as she could. Her behaviour was noted by me; I looked at her as well and thanked her graciously. Once, during late winter, I was riding from Fontainebleau to Paris, and as I came up over the little bridge she stepped out of her shop door and said to me as I rode by: "Your servant, Sir!" I returned her greeting and as I looked back from time to time, saw she had leaned out further so as to follow me with her eyes as long as possible. I had a servant and a postilion behind me whom I intended to send back to Fontainebleau that same evening with letters to certain ladies. On my orders the servant dismounted and went over to the young woman to tell her my name and that I had noted her inclination to see and to greet me; I would, if she wished to know me better, visit her wherever she desired.

She answered my servant that he could not have brought her a more welcome message; she would come to wherever I invited her.

In riding on I asked my servant whether he perhaps knew a place where I could meet with the woman. He answered that he would conduct her to a certain procuress; but since he was a most caring and conscientious person, this servant Wilhelm of Courtrai, he added at once: since the plague had surfaced here and there and not only those of the lower, dirty members of the public but also a doctor and a Canon had already died of it, he advised me to have mattresses, blankets and bedlinen brought from home. I accepted the proposal and he promised to prepare a decent bed for me. Before dismounting, I said he should also fetch a decent wash-basin to the place, a small bottle of aromatic essence and some pastries and apples; in addition he was to see to it that the room was well heated, for it was so cold that my feet were frozen stiff in the stirrups and the sky was heavy with snow-clouds.

That same evening I went there and found a very beautiful woman of about twenty sitting on the bed, while the procuress, her head and rounded back wrapped in a black shawl, addressed her in eager tones. The door stood ajar and great fresh logs blazed noisily in the fireplace; they did not hear me approach and I remained for an instant standing in the doorway. The young woman was calmly gazing into the flames with wide eyes; with one movement of the head she had, as it were, distanced herself by miles from the revolting old crone; in so doing some tresses of her heavy dark hair had tumbled from beneath the little night-cap she wore and fell curling into a number of natural locks over her shift between shoulder and breast. She was still wearing a short petticoat made of green woollen material and slippers on her feet. At that moment I must have betrayed my presence by some noise: she abruptly veered round and turned towards me a face whose surpassing intensity might have evoked an almost wild expression but for the radiant surrender which streamed from the wide open eyes and burst from her speechless mouth like an invisible flame. She appealed to me immensely; quicker than the blink of an eye the old crone was out of the room and I beside my girlfriend. When in the first intoxication of surprised possession I wished to avail myself of some liberties, she withdrew with an indescribably vital urgency of both glance and deep-toned voice. But in the next moment I felt myself embraced by her as she clung to me more fervently still with a constant yearning glance of those insatiable eyes, no less than with lips and arms; yet then again it seemed that she wished to speak but those lips tremulous with kisses did not form words, the trembling throat produced no clearer sound than that of broken sobbing.

Now I had spent a great part of that day on horse-back upon frosty country roads; thereafter I experienced a most annoying and bad-tempered scene in the King's antechamber and later, in order to quell my bad temper, took a stiff drink as well as fenced hard with a two-hander; so amidst this charming and mysterious adventure, while I lay there with soft arms about my neck and covered by fragrant tresses, I was overcome by such sudden, acute fatigue that I could no longer recall how I came to enter that particular room; indeed for an instant

I even confused the lady whose heart beat so close to mine with quite another from earlier days, and fell asleep immediately after.

When I woke again it was still darkest night but I sensed at once that my girlfriend was no longer at my side. I raised my head and saw by the feeble light of the extinguishing embers that she was standing by the window: she had pushed open one shutter and was look-ing out through the aperture. Then she turned around, noticed that I was awake and cried out (I can still see how she lifted the ball of her left hand up to her cheek and cast over her shoulder the hair that had tumbled down) : "It's a long time until day-break, a long time!" Only now did I see how tall and beautiful she was, and could barely wait for the moment when, with a few calm long steps of those lovely feet illumined by the reddish glow, she was at my side once more. But she first stepped over to the fire, bent to the ground, took up the last heavy log lying outside into her radiant naked arms and quickly threw it on the embers. She then turned round, her face sparkled with flames and joy; she snatched an apple from the table in hurrying past and was beside me at once, her limbs still suffused by the fresh glow of the fire, and then quickly relaxed and permeated by fiercer flames from within, she embraced me with her right arm and with her left offered my mouth at once the cool, bitten fruit, cheeks, lips and eyes. The last log in the hearth burned brighter than all the rest. Spurting out sparks it sucked in the flame, then made it flare up fiercely so that the fiery glow burst over us like a wave breaking against the wall; it lifted high our entwined shadows and then let them sink down again. The tough timber repeatedly crackled nourishing from within ever new flames, its tongues flickering up and dispelling the deep gloom with spurts and cones of reddish lights. However the flame suddenly sank down, a cold gust of wind silently opened the shutter as though by hand and exposed the barren, repellent twilight.

We sat up and knew now that day had dawned. But that out there was unlike any other day. It was quite unlike the awakening of the earth. What lay outside there did not resemble a street. Nothing individual could be recognized: it was a cloudless, insubstantial tumult wherein timeless masks would appear to be in motion. From somewhere far away, as if from memory, a church clock sounded and damp, cold air which belonged to no hour, wafted in ever more strongly so that we huddled together shuddering. She leaned back and fixed her eyes with all her might on my face; her throat jerked, something was forced up and swelled to the tip of her lips; it did not form a word or a sigh or a kiss, but something unborn which was akin to all three. It grew brighter from one moment to the next and the manifold expression of her twitching face became ever more expressive; suddenly dragging footsteps and voices from outside passed so close to the window that she ducked down and turned her face to the wall. It was two men who passed by: for a second the beam of a little lantern carried by one of them was cast inside; the other man was pushing a barrow with a wheel that creaked and groaned. When they had passed I stood up, closed the shutter and lit a candle. Half an apple lay there still: together we ate it and then I asked her if I could see her once more since I was only going to travel on Sunday. This, however, had been the night between Thursday and Friday.

She replied that she definitely desired this even more than I did: however, if I did not remain for the whole of Sunday she would find it impossible since she could only meet me again in the night between Sunday to Monday.

First a number of obstacles occurred to me, so that I created a number of difficulties to which she listened without a word but with an intensely pained, questioning look and at the same time an almost uncanny hardening and darkening of her features. At this I immediately promised that I would of course remain on the Sunday and added that I would arrive at the same place on Sunday then. On hearing these words she looked steadily at me and said in a fairly rough and faltering tone to her voice: "I know perfectly well that for your sake I have come to a shameful house; but I did so of my own free will because I wanted to be with you, because I would have agreed to any condition. But now I feel as though I were the last and lowest of streetwalkers if I were to come back here a second time. I did it for your sake because to me you are who you are: because you are Bassompierre, because you are the one person in this world who by his presence makes this house honourable for me!" She said "house"; and for a moment it seemed as if a despicable word was on her tongue; in pronouncing this word she cast such a glance on these four walls, on this bed, on the blanket that had slid down onto the floor, that beneath the beam of light which shot from her eyes all these ugly and brutish things seemed to recoil and cower before her as if the wretched room had indeed grown larger in that instant.

She then added in an indescribably gentle and solemn tone: "may I die a miserable death if I ever belonged to or desired any other man on earth besides my husband and you!" With half-open, life-breathing lips slightly lowered she seemed to expect some kind of reply, some assurance of my belief; yet unable to glean from my face what she desired, for her intense searching look clouded over, her eyelashes flickered, and all of a sudden she was at the window, her back turned on me, her forehead pressed with full force against the shutter, her whole body so shaken with silent but terribly violent weeping, that words died in my mouth and I dared not touch her. At last I took hold of one of her hands which hung as though lifeless, and with the most insistent words suggested by the moment I at length succeeded in so far pacifying her that she once again turned her tear-stained face towards me; then suddenly a smile broke out like a light from her eyes and about her lips and consumed all traces of weeping in a moment as it flooded her whole face with radiance. Now it turned into the most charming form of play as she once more began to speak to me, beginning with the sentence: "You wish to see me once more? Then I shall introduce you at my aunt's!" This was endlessly varied, the first half spoken tenfold, now with sweet urgency, now with childishly acted mistrust, then the second part was first whispered into my ear as the greatest secret, then tossed over her shoulder with a shrug and pouted lips as the most self-evident assignation in all the world, and finally repeated to my face as she hung on me laughing and flattering. She described the house to me in greatest detail, just as a child is told the way when it is to cross the street alone for the first time to go to the baker's. Then she straightened up, grew serious – and she directed the whole might of her radiant eyes towards me with such force that it seemed they would have the power to draw even a dead creature to them – then continued: "I shall expect you between ten o'clock and midnight and later still, and constantly, and the door downstairs will be open. First you'll come to a small passage, but don't delay there, for my aunt's door faces this. Then you'll come to a stairs that leads to the first floor and that's where I am!" And while she closed her eyes as though dizzy, she threw back her head, spread her arms and embraced me; then she was quickly out of my arms and dressed in her clothes, distant and serious and out of the room; for now it was broad daylight.

I made my arrangements, sent some of my servants ahead with my things and already felt such acute impatience on the following evening that not long after the angelus bell I crossed the little bridge with my servant Wilhelm, whom I had ordered not to bring a lamp, so as to catch at least a glimpse of my girlfriend in her shop or in the adjacent apartment, and give her some sort of sign of my presence even though I had little hope of anything more than to exchange a few words with her.

So as not to draw attention I remained standing on the bridge and sent my servant ahead to sound out any opportunity. He was absent for a considerable time and on his return wore that dejected, brooding expression I always noted on this good fellow whenever he was unable to successfully execute any orders of mine. "The shop is locked up", he said, "and also there's no one around, it seems. At any rate, no one at all is to be seen or heard in the rooms facing the street. You could only climb into the yard over a high wall; besides, a large dog is there growling. But one of the front rooms is lit up, and you can see into the shop through a crack; only a pity it's empty."

Feeling disgruntled, I was about to turn back but then slowly stalked past the house just the same, when my servant in his zeal again put an eye to the aperture through which a glimmer of light passed and whispered to me that, true enough, the woman was not in the room but the husband now certainly was. Being curious to see this shopkeeper, whom I could not remember ever having seen in his shop even once, and whom I imagined by turns to be a misshapen, fat individual or a skinny, frail old man, I stepped up to the window and was wholly astounded to see an unusually tall and well-built man walking around in the well-appointed, panelled room. He was certainly a head taller than myself and when he turned round revealed a very beautiful, deeply serious face with a brown beard which showed a few silver threads and a brow of uncommon nobility, such that his temples formed a broader expanse than I had ever observed on any human being. Although he was quite alone in the room his glance was unsettled, his lips moved, and whilst walking up and down and occasionally halting, he seemed to be engaged in imaginary conversation with another person. In one instance he moved his arm as though waving away a reply with half-indulgent superiority. Each of his gestures displayed great casualness and almost disdainful pride and I could not help recalling, as he moved about in his solitary way, the vivid image of a most exalted prisoner I had to guard in the King's service during his captivity in a turret cell of Blois Castle. The similarity appeared to me to become still greater when the man raised his right hand and looked down at his bent-up fingers most attentively, indeed with grim severity.

For I had seen this same exalted prisoner often gazing at a ring he wore on the index finger of the right hand, and from which he never parted, with much the same gesture. The man in the room then stepped up to the table, pushed the water-bowl in front of the candle and brought both hands into the circle of light with fingers outstretched: he appeared to be scrutinizing his nails. He then blew out the candle, went out of the room, leaving me in something of a dull, angry mood of jealousy, since the desire for his wife continued to grow within me like a fire that spreads, consuming everything I encountered and so was fed in a confused way by this unexpected appearance; just as though every snowflake were now dispersed by a damp cold and stayed clinging and melting singly on my eyebrows and cheeks.

I spent the next day in the most futile manner, paid no proper attention to any form of activity, bought a horse which I actually did not like, waited on the Duke of

Nemours after dinner and spent a little time there gaming and in the most trivial and obnoxious conversations. It so happened that the talk touched on nothing other than the plague which was spreading ever more vigorously through the town, and one was incapable of exacting any other word from all these nobles than similar stories about the hasty burial of corpses, of straw fires that had to be lit in the death chambers to consume the poisonous vapours and so forth; the silliest figure to my mind, however, was the Canon of Chandieu who, though portly and hale as ever, could not forbear incessantly squinting down at his fingernails to see if that suspicious turning blue was already showing by which the sickness is usually announced.

I was revolted by all this, returned home early and went to bed but could not sleep, dressed again out of impatience and was determined, whatever the cost, to go back to see my girlfriend even if I had to enter by force with those who serve me. I went over to the window to rouse my servants; the icy night air brought me to my senses and I realized that this would be the surest way to ruin everything. Still dressed I threw myself onto the bed and at last fell asleep.

I spent the Sunday until evening in similar fashion, was much too early in the appointed street, but forced myself to walk up and down in a neighbouring lane until it struck ten o'clock. I then found the house and the door she had described to me and also saw that the door was open, while beyond it lay the passage and the stairs. The second door above, however, to which the stairs led was locked and yet it let a slender strip of light shine through from below. So she was inside waiting and was perhaps standing behind the door listening, just as I was outside. I scratched with my nail at the door and then heard footsteps inside: they seemed to me hesitant, unsure footsteps of naked feet. I stood for a time holding my breath and then I began to knock: but I heard a man's voice which asked me who was outside there. I pressed myself into the darkness of the doorway and made no sound: the door remained shut and I climbed in uttermost silence step by step down the stairs, crept along the passage out into the open and paced with throbbing temples and clenched teeth, burning with impatience, up and down a few streets. Finally I was drawn back again to the house: I did not as yet wish to enter; I felt, I knew she would send the man away, it had to succeed, I would come to her very soon. The lane was narrow: there was no house on the opposite side but the wall of a convent garden: I kept close along this and tried to guess the window from across the way. There, in an open window of the upper storey a light flickered and faded again as though from a flame. I now believed I could see everything before me: she had thrown a large log onto the fire, just as before, she now stood as before in the middle of the room, her limbs sparkling from the flames, or she sat on the bed listening and waiting. I would see her from the door and the shadow of her neck, her shoulders, which the transparent wave raised and lowered. Now I was in the passage, now on the stairs; and now the door was no longer locked: being ajar, it also allowed the flicker of light through from the side.

Now I stretched out my hand for the door-handle, when I thought I could hear footsteps inside and the voices of several others. I did not want to believe it though: I took it for the surging of blood in my temples, in my throat, and for the blazing fire inside. Then too it had blazed aloud. Now that I had taken hold of the door-handle I was compelled to grasp that there were people inside, a number of people. But now it was all the same to me: I felt, I knew, she too was inside, and as soon as I pushed open the door I could see her, seize her, and even if it was from the grasp of others, drag her to me with one arm, even if I had to hew a space with my sword for her, with my dagger, out of a throng of screaming people! The only thing that seemed unbearable to me was to wait any longer.

I pushed open the door and saw: a number of people in the middle of an empty room who were burning bedding straw and by the light of a flame which illuminated the entire room, scraping down walls, with debris lying on the floor, and along one wall a table upon which two naked bodies lay stretched out, one very large, its head covered, the other smaller, stretched straight out by the wall, and alongside the black shadow of its shape as it rose and fell.

I tottered down the stairs and ran into two grave-diggers in front of the house: one of them raised his little lantern to my face and asked me what I was looking for; the other pushed his groaning, creaking barrow up towards the front door of the house. I drew my sword so as to keep them at bay and came back home. I at once drank three or four large glasses of strong wine and having rested, set off on the following day on my journey to Lothringen.

All efforts made by me on my return to discover anything at all about this woman were in vain. I even visited the shop with the two angels; however, the people who now owned it did not know who had kept it before them.

M. de Bassompierre, *Journal de ma vie*,

Cologne 1663.

Goethe, *Conversations of German Emigrés*.

LUCIDOR

FIGURES FOR AN UNWRITTEN COMEDY

Frau von Murska occupied a small apartment in an inner-city hotel towards the end of the eighteen-nineties. She possessed a lesser-known and yet not altogether obscure name of the nobility; from her accounts it was assumed that a family seat in the Russian sector of Poland that by right belonged to her and her children was, for the time being, on legal grounds sequestered or otherwise withheld from its rightful owners. She appeared for the moment embarrassed, but only for the moment. With a grown-up daughter Arabella, a half-grown son Lucidor, and an aged lady's maid, she occupied three bedrooms and a drawing-room with windows looking out over the Kärntnerstrasse. Here she kept a number of family portraits, copper engravings and miniatures pinned to the walls, a piece of old satin with embroidered crest set upon a guéridon and also a couple of silver jugs and baskets, all good eighteenth-century French work; and this is where she received guests. She had sent off letters, paid visits and since she had any number of "attachments" in all directions, a sort of salon was fairly quickly established. It was one of those somewhat vague salons which, all according to the strictness of those who assessed, are judged to be "possible" or "impossible". All the same, Frau von Murska was anything but vulgar and not at all boring, and the daughter was of still more pronounced distinction in her nature and demeanour and she was extraordinarily beautiful. If you arrived between four and six, you could be sure of finding the mother and almost never without company; the daughter was not always to be seen, and the thirteen or fourteen year-old Lucidor was known only to intimates.

Frau von Murska was a truly cultivated woman and her education had nothing banal about it. Within Viennese high society, to which she vaguely felt she belonged without entering into more than peripheral contact with it, she would have been hard challenged to maintain the status of a "blue-stocking". But in her head there existed such a conglomeration of experiences, conjectures, presentiments, errors, enthusiasms, incidents, apprehensions, that it was not worth the effort to persist in what she had gleaned from books. Her conversation galloped from one subject to the next and found the most improbable transitions; her restlessness could arouse sympathy – when you listened to her speak, you knew without her needing to mention it, that she suffered from insomnia to the point of madness and that she was consumed by cares, conjectures and shattered hopes – yet it was certainly amusing and truly remarkable to listen to her, and without wishing to be indiscreet, she was so on occasion to a most appalling degree. In short, she was a simpleton but of the more agreeable variety. She was a good soul and basically a charming and by no means ordinary woman. But her complicated life, to which she was unequal, had brought her such confusion that already in her forty-second year she had become a fantastical figure. Most of her judgements, her concepts, were peculiar and of great inner refinement; yet they almost always had the most improbable point of reference and in no wise applied to the person or relationship concerned at the time. The closer a person stood to her, the less she overlooked him; and it would have contradicted every rule if she had not harboured in her mind the most wrong-headed image of her two children and acted blindly in accordance with it. Arabella was in her eyes an angel, Lucidor a hard little thing with little heart in him. Arabella was a thousand times too good for this world and Lucidor fitted into this world quite exceptionally. In reality Arabella was the very image of her deceased father: that of a proud, dissatisfied, impatient and very beautiful person, who was quick to despise but disguised his disdain in quite extraordinary manner, was respected or envied by men and loved by many women and was possessed of an arid mental disposition. Little Lucidor, by contrast, was pure heart. But I would rather state at this juncture that Lucidor was not a young gentleman but a girl who was called Lucile. The idea of having the younger daughter appear as a transvestite for the duration of the stay in Vienna had, like all Frau von Murska's ideas, come to her like a flash of lightening, yet so had the most complicated ulterior issues and concatenations. Here above all it involved the thought of making a most ingenious chess move against an old, mysterious but thankfully in fact existing uncle who lived in Vienna and for whose sake – all these hopes and conjectures were utterly vague – she had perhaps chosen just this city for her residence. At the same time the disguise had some added, quite real, and most immediately evident advantages. It was easier to live with one daughter rather than two of not quite the same age; for the girls were after all almost four years apart; one could thus get by at somewhat lesser expense. Moreover it was a still better, more appropriate position for Arabella to be the only daughter, than the elder one; and the rather pretty little "brother", a sort of groom, threw this lovely being into further relief.

A number of accidental circumstances proved fortu- itous: Frau von Murska's ideas were never fully grounded in reality, they merely linked in a peculiar manner the actual, the given, and that which in her fancy seemed possible or attainable. Five years ago it was found neces- sary to shorten Lucile's lovely hair – at the time, still an eleven year-old child, she was contending with typhus. Furthermore Lucile preferred riding astride; this was a habit that stemmed from the time she had ridden the estate horses bareback to the watering-place together with the Little Russian peasant lads. Lucile accepted the disguise just as she might have accepted many other things. Her mental make-up was patient and even the most absurd things can quite readily become habit. In addition, since she was painfully shy, she delighted in the thought that she need never appear in the drawing-room and have to play the pubescent girl. The old lady's maid was the sole person privy to the secret; strangers found nothing amiss. No one is readily the first to discern something suspicious: for it is not generally given to mankind to see things as they are. Lucile also had genuinely boyish narrow hips and nothing else besides that might all too easily betray the girl. In fact the matter remained undisclosed, indeed unsuspected, and when that turn of events came about which made of little Lucidor a bride or something yet more feminine, all the world was astounded.

Naturally such a beautiful and in every sense good-looking young person as Arabella did not long remain without a few more or less declared suitors. Amongst these Vladimir was by far the most significant. He was supremely good-looking and had quite exceptionally beautiful hands. He was more than wealthy and wholly independent, without parents, without siblings. His father had been a middle-class Austrian officer; his mother stemmed from a very well-known Baltic family. Amongst all those who associated with Arabella, he was the only truly serious "match". In addition there was another quite special circumstance that truly enchanted Frau von Murska. It so happened that just he was linked through certain family connections with that uncle who was so difficult to deal with, so inaccessible and so extremely important; that uncle for whose sake they were actually living in Vienna and Lucile had become Lucidor. This uncle, who occupied an entire floor of the Palais Buquoy in the Wallnerstrasse and was at the same time a much talked-of gentleman, had received Frau von Murska very poorly. Though she was in actual fact the widow of his nephew (more precisely: the grandson of his brother's father) she had only been able to see him on her third visit and since then had never once been invited even to breakfast or to a cup of tea. On the other hand he had, de mauvaise grâce, once permitted that Lucidor be conveyed to him. It was a peculiarity on the part of the interesting old gentleman that he could not abide women, either old or young. But then the uncertain hope remained that he might at some time conceive a consummate interest in a young gentleman who was, after all, a blood relation even though he was not a bearer of the same name. And even this most uncertain hope was of infinite value in a highly precarious situation. Now Lucidor, at his mother's behest, had indeed travelled over alone but not been accepted, about which Lucidor was very happy, his mother, however, was quite devastated especially since nothing further ensued and the precious thread appeared to be severed. Now Vladimir by virtue of his twofold relationship appeared to be the providential man to reconnect it once more. To get the thing going again Lucidor was at times inconspicuously brought into play whenever Vladimir visited mother and daughter; and chance was propitious in that Vladimir took a liking to the lad and at their very first meeting invited him to ride out with him on occasion, which after a rapid exchange of glances between Arabella and her mother was gratefully accepted. Vladimir's liking for the younger brother of a person with whom he had wholeheartedly fallen in love was all too understandable; and besides, there is scarcely anything more agreeable than a glance of unreserved admiration from the eyes of a nice fourteen year-old youngster.

Frau von Murska was increasingly on her knees before Vladimir. Arabella grew impatient at this as with most of her mother's attitudes and almost involuntarily, although she was glad to see Vladimir, she began to flirt with one of his rivals, Herr von Imfanger, a pleasant and quite elegant Tirolean, half farmer, half gentleman, but who was simply out of the question as a contender. Once when the mother dared to utter some mild reproaches that Arabella did not behave towards Vladimir as he had a right to expect, Arabella gave a dismissive reply which contained much more disdain and coldness vis-a-vis Vladimir than she in fact felt. Lucidor-Lucile was by chance present. The blood shot to her heart and surged from it again. A piercing sensation flashed through her: she felt fear, anger and pain all at once. She felt dull astonishment at her sister. Arabella was always strange to her. At that moment she appeared almost gruesome and she could not have said if she admired or hated her. Then everything dissolved into boundless suffering. She went out and locked herself in her room. If she had been told that she simply loved Vladimir she might not have understood this. She acted as she had to, automatically, while the tears streamed down, the true meaning of which she did not understand. She sat down and wrote an ardent love letter to Vladimir: yet not for herself, for Arabella. The fact that her handwriting was the very image of Arabella's had often annoyed her. She had forced herself to adopt another quite ugly handwriting. But she could make use of the earlier one, which suited her hand, at any time. Indeed she found it easier to write like that. The letter was such as can only be penned by those who are devoid of thought and are actually beside themselves. It disavowed Arabella's entire nature: but that was just what it wished to do, what it was supposed to do. It was most improbable, but then again in a certain way probable as the expression of a violent inner revolution. Had Arabella been able to love deeply and with abandon and become conscious of this all at once in a sudden breakthrough, she might then have been able to express herself in this way and to speak with such boldness and fervent disdain of herself, of the Arabella whom everyone knew. The letter was strange, and yet not wholly improbable as the letter of a passionate girl who was quite unpredictable. For the man in love, the woman he loves is always an unpredictable being. And when all is said and done, it was the kind of letter which a man in his position would always secretly wish for and hope to receive. Here I must anticipate that the letter was in fact received by Vladimir: this actually happened on the very next afternoon upon the stairs with Lucidor creeping up, cautiously calling out and whispering as the excited, clumsy and presumed postillon d'amour on behalf of his beautiful sister. A postscript was of course added: it contained the urgent, indeed imploring request not to be angry if merely the slightest change in Arabella's behaviour either towards the beloved, or even towards others, might not be discernible. He was also most fervently implored not to betray by any word, not even by a glance, that he knew he was most tenderly loved.

A few days pass in which Vladimir only briefly meets with Arabella, and then never in private. He meets her in the way she had demanded it; she meets him in the manner he had predicted. He feels both happy and unhappy. He only knows how fond of her he is. The situation is such as to make him boundlessly impatient. Lucidor, with whom he now rides out daily, and in whose company almost alone he feels at ease, notices with delight and terror the changes in his friend's manner; the growing intensity of his impatience. There follows another letter, if anything more tender than the first, a renewed touching plea not to disturb the much threatened happiness of this delicate situation, to let these confessions suffice and to reply at best in writing via Lucidor. A letter now passes this way and that every second or third day. Vladimir has days of happiness and so does Lucidor. The tone between them has now changed; they possess an inexhaustible topic of conversation. Whenever they have dismounted in some coppice in the Prater and Lucidor has handed over his latest letter, he observes the features of the reader with anxious pleasure. Sometimes he asks questions that are almost indiscreet; but the excitement of the young boy who is entangled in this love affair and his cleverness – some secret thing that makes him daily prettier and more delicate – amuses Vladimir, and he has to admit to himself, withdrawn and proud as he generally is, that he is hard put not to speak with Lucidor about Arabella. Lucidor also poses as the misogynist, the little, precocious youngster who is cynical in a childish way. What he proffers is by no means banal; for he knows how to mix in some element of what doctors call "introspective truths". Yet Vladimir, who is not lacking in self-esteem, can instruct him that the love he inspires, and which he inspires in such a being as Arabella, is made up of a distinctive quality comparable to nothing else. Lucidor finds

Vladimir all the more admirable at such moments and himself petty and pitiful. They touch on marriage and this subject is a torment to Lucidor, for then Vladimir is exclusively preoccupied with the real-life Arabella instead of the Arabella of the letters. Furthermore Lucidor fears like death itself any decision, any incisive change. His only thought is simply to prolong the situation. It is hard to express what resources the poor soul conjures up so as to keep the outwardly and inwardly precarious situation for days and weeks in some kind of fragile balance: he lacks the strength to think beyond that. Since he has after all been given the mission to gain something for the family from the uncle, he does his level best. Sometimes Vladimir accompanies him; the uncle is a strange old gentleman who is evidently amused at not needing to feel any constraint vis-à-vis younger folk, and his conversation is such that an hour of this kind represents a truly agonizing little test for Lucidor. Meanwhile nothing seems to lie further from the old man's mind than having to do something for his relatives. Lucidor is incapable of lying and wishes more than anything to console his mother. On his mother's part, the deeper all hopes sink which she had placed on the uncle, sees with still greater impatience that nothing between Arabella and Vladimir appears to be approaching a decision. The wretched people on whom she is dependent in the matter of funds, begin to consign the one or other of these splendid prospects to her debit account as a failed investment. Her fear, her anxiously hidden impatience is made known to everyone, most of all to poor Lucidor, through whose head these incompatible matters pass in confusion. But he is yet to receive some subtler and keener lessons within the strange school of life to which he has now been committed.

The term "double nature" in relation to Arabella had never expressly been used. But the concept suggested itself: the Arabella of daytime was defensive, coquettish, precise, self-assured worldly and curt almost to excess; the Arabella of night-time who wrote to her lover by candlelight was devoted, almost boundlessly desirous. By chance or by dint of destiny, this also corresponded to a secret division in Vladimir's nature. He too possessed, like every animate being, more or less his day and night side. A somewhat arid pride, an ambition without lowness and avidness but one that was resolute and permanent, were opposed to other impulses or rather not opposed, but cowered in darkness, sought to hide, were ever ready to plunge down beneath the dim threshold into the semi-conscious. A fanciful sensuality which could, as it were, dream itself even into an animal, into a dog, or a swan, had at times taken complete command of his soul. He did not like to recall those times of transition from boyhood to youth. But something of this remained in him always, and this abandoned night side of his being, hardly brushed by a thought and wilfully neglected, was now touched by a dark, mysterious light: the love of that other, invisible Arabella . Had this Arabella of the day chanced to be his wife or become his lover, he would always have remained down-to-earth with her and would never have conceded and allowed any space in his existence to phantasms from a child-hood wilfully suppressed. He also thought in different terms of the woman who dwelt in the dark and wrote to her in a different way. What was Lucidor to do when his friend wished to receive something more, some vital sign, rather than these lines upon white paper? Lucidor was alone with his trepidation, his confusion, his love. The Arabella of the daytime did not help him. Indeed it seemed, as though driven by some demon, she was acting against him. The colder, more erratic, worldlier, more coquettish she was, the more Vladimir hoped and begged of the other one. He begged so well that Lucidor did not find the courage to refuse. Had he found it, his tender pen would not have found the turn of phrase to express a refusal. Then came a night in which Vladimir was permitted to think he would be received by Arabella in Lucidor's room, and how he would be received. Lucidor had somehow succeeded in so completely darkening the window towards the Kärntnerstrasse that you could not see your hand before your eyes. That voices needed to be hushed to barely audible whispers was clear: just an ordi-nary door divided them from the lady-in-waiting. Where Lucidor spent the night remained undisclosed: yet he was apparently not privy to the secret and some useful excuse had been used towards him. It was strange that Arabella wore her lovely hair bound up tightly in a thick scarf and refused to allow her friend's hand gently but firmly from untying the scarf. Yet this was almost the only thing she did refuse. Several nights passed that did not resemble this night, but there followed another night which did resemble it and Vladimir was very happy. Perhaps these were the happiest days of his entire life. The assurance of his nocturnal joy inspires him with a special tone towards Arabella when he is with her during the day. He gains special pleasure from the fact that she is so unaccountably different at daytime; her powerful self-command, that she never once forgets herself even in a glance or a movement, has something enchanting about it. He thinks he can notice that she grows all the colder towards him from week to week the tenderer she has shown herself to be in the nights. At all events he wishes to be no less adept, to appear no less controlled. In totally submitting himself to this mysteriously strong female will, he believes that he may in some measure deserve his nocturnal joys. He begins to derive the most powerful pleasure especially from her dual nature. The fact that she, who in no way appears to be his, belongs to him, that the same woman who can give herself unreservedly is also able to assert herself with such an untouched, untouchable presence, is an intoxicating experience like the repeated draught of a magic potion. He acknowledges that he must thank destiny on bended knee to be favoured in so unique a way, and in a manner subtly gleaned from the secret of his nature. He expresses this with overflowing heart both to himself and to Lucidor. There is nothing which could arouse deadlier dread in poor Lucidor's innermost being.

Meanwhile Arabella, the true one, has so decidedly turned away from Vladimir in these weeks, that he would surely have noticed it hour by hour had he not had the strangest urge to wrongly interpret everything. Even though he does not actually give himself away, she senses something between herself and him which did not exist before. She had always felt some mutual understanding, and she still has an understanding with him; her day sides are all alike; they might yet conduct a good marriage of convenience. She had no understanding with Herr von Imfanger, but she likes him. She now feels more strongly that Vladimir does not appeal to her in this sense; that inexplicable something which seems to vibrate from him to her makes her impatient. It is not courtship, nor is it flattery; she cannot be clear about what it is but she does not relish it. Imfanger clearly must know that he appeals to her. Vladimir on his part believes he has altogether different kinds of proof on the matter. A most peculiar situation arises between the two young gentlemen. Each of them thinks the other has every reason to be down-hearted or simply to abandon the chase. Each finds both the attitude and the blithe good mood of the other at bottom simply ludicrous. Neither knows what to make of the other and each considers the other a downright fop and a fool.

The mother is in the most painful situation. Several sources of information dry up. Personal friends leave her in the lurch. A loan proffered under the mask of friendship is ruthlessly called in. Vehement decisions are ever close to Frau von Murska's heart. She is about to break up her household in Vienna from one day to the next, take leave of her acquaintances by letter, seek asylum somewhere, even though it be on the sequestered estate in the manager's family home. Arabella does not receive such a decision in good grace, yet despair is foreign to her nature. Lucidor has anxiously to conceal within him a true, boundless form of despair. Several nights have passed without her having summoned her friend. She wished to call him again this very night. The evening conversation between Arabella and her mother, the decision on departure, the impossibility of preventing departure: all this strikes her like a hammer blow. And should she take desperate measures, throw everything to the winds, confess everything to her mother, above all reveal to her friend who the Arabella of his nights had been; fear of his disappointment and his anger pierces her with an icy chill. She feels like a criminal, but only towards him, she does not consider the others. She cannot see him on this night. She feels she would die of shame, fear and confusion. Instead of holding him in her arms, she writes to him for the last time. It is the humblest, most moving letter, and nothing is less suited to it than the name Arabella with which she signs it. She had never hoped to become his wife. To live with him just a few years, even for one year as his mistress would be infinite happiness. But even that may not and cannot be. He should not ask, not press her on this, she implores him. He should come once more tomorrow to visit, but only towards evening. As for the day after that – perhaps they will already have left on their journey. One day perhaps he may learn, understand, she wishes to add: forgive, but the word seems inconceivable to her in Arabella's mouth, and so she does not write it. She sleeps little, gets up early, sends the letter to Vladimir via the hotel porter. The morning is passed with packing up. After lunch, without mentioning anything, she travels over to the uncle. The idea came to her during the night. She would find the words, the arguments to mollify the old fellow. A miracle could happen and those tightly closed purse strings would open up. She does not consider the hard reality of these things, only of her mother, of the situation, of her love. With the money or the letter in her hand she would fall down at her mother's feet and beg as her sole reward – for what? – her exhausted, tormented brain almost fails her – yes! For what goes without saying: that they remain in Vienna, that everything stays as it is. She finds her uncle at home. The details of their scene, which takes a rather strange turn, are not to be told here. Only this: she does indeed soften his heart – he is close to doing the decisive deed, but a petty senile whim overturns the decision once more: he will do something later; when precisely, he does not declare, and there's an end. She travels home, creeps up the stairs and into her room; between boxes and suitcases, squatting on the floor she abandons herself utterly to despair. There she thinks she can hear Vladimir's voice in the drawing-room. She creeps up on tiptoe and listens. It really is Vladimir – with Arabella, who with rather raised voices are engaged in the strangest dialogue.

Vladimir has received Arabella's mysterious letter of farewell in the course of the morning. Never has anything found his heart in such a way. He feels that something shadowy stands between him and her, but not between heart and heart. He feels within him the love and the strength to discover, to understand, to forgive whatever it may be. He loves the incomparable lover of his nights too dearly to be able to live without her. Strangely, he does not think of the real Arabella at all; it seems almost odd to him that this is the woman he needs to confront, to assuage, to raise up, to win completely and for ever. He arrives and finds the mother alone in the drawing-room. She is as excited, confused and fantastic as ever. He is different from any other time she had seen him. He kisses her hands and speaks only in a deeply touched, reserved manner. He asks her to permit him a private conversation with Arabella. Frau von Murska is delighted and instantly in seventh heaven. The improbable is her true element. She hastens to fetch Arabella; she urges her not to refuse the noble young man now, as everything has taken such a marvellous turn. Arabella is immensely astonished. "I am simply not on that footing with him," she says coldly. "One never suspects what footing there is with men," the mother replies and sends her into the drawing-room. Vladimir is embarrassed, deeply moved and ardent. Arabella increasingly finds that Herr von Imfanger is right in seeing Vladimir as an odd fellow. Vladimir, having lost control through her coldness, pleads with her finally to drop her mask. Arabella has no idea whatsoever what is to be dropped. Vladimir becomes both tender and angry at the same time, a mixture which Arabella relishes so little that she finally rushes out of the room and leaves him standing there. Vladimir in his utter amazement is that much closer to considering her insane, as she had just then suggested to him that she considers him no less so, and was of one opinion on this point with a third party. At that moment Vladimir would have held a most baffled monologue if the outer door had not opened and the oddest apparition had not dashed towards him, embraced him and slid down from him to the ground. It is Lucidor, and then again not Lucidor but Lucile, a sweet girl bathed in tears, wearing Arabella's morning dress, her boyish short hair disguised by a thick silk scarf. It is his friend and familiar, and at the same time his mysterious girlfriend, his beloved, his wife. A dialogue such as now took shape may be brought about by life, and comedy may attempt to emulate it, but never a short story.

Whether Lucidor later actually became Vladimir's wife or remained in daytime and in another country what she had been in the darkness of night, namely his happy lover, might equally be left unwritten here.

It may be doubted whether Vladimir was a sufficiently worthy human being to deserve so much devotion. But in any event, the entire beauty of an unreservedly devoted soul like that of Lucile could never have revealed itself under other than these extraordinary circumstances.

A LETTER

This is the letter written by Philipp Lord Chandos, younger son of the Earl of Bath, to Francis Bacon, later Lord Verulam and Viscount St. Albans, being an apology to his friend for his total withdrawal from all literary activity. It is most generous of you, my honoured friend, to overlook my total silence over two years and to write to me as you did.

It is more than generous of you to mark your concern about me, your perplexity at the mental torpor into which I appear to you to be declining, by an expression of levity and wit which only great men command such as are deeply versed in the perils of life and yet remain undaunted.

You close with the aphorism by Hippocrates: "*Qui grave mordo correpti dolores non sentient, iis mens aegrotat*", and you say that I have no need of medication to conquer my affliction but, even more, to sharpen the sense of my inner condition. I wish to answer you in the manner you merit, wish to open my innermost self to you, yet do not know how I might bring this about. I scarcely know if I am still the same man to whom your precious letter is addressed; am I really that person, now twenty-six years of age, who at nineteen could lightly toss off the "New Paris", the "Dream of Daphne", the "Epithalamium"; all those pastoral plays dizzy with the delirious splendour of their diction, which a heaven-sent Queen and some all-too indulgent Lords and Gentlemen are still gracious enough to remember? Am I still the one who at twenty-three made the inward discovery of the complex of Latin periods beneath the stony arcades of the Great Square in Venice, whose mental blueprint and structure called forth greater inward rapture than any buildings rising from the sea by Palladio and Sansovino? And could I, if otherwise one and the same person, have so fully expunged from my inscrutable self all traces and scars of this issue of my most strenuous thought, that the title of the little tract named in your letter lying before me stares back at me as a thing cold and alien? So much so indeed, that I was unable to grasp it at once as a familiar pattern of organized words, but could only understand it word by word as though I had encountered these Latin terms, thus connected, for the very first time. However, I remain myself after all, and rhetoric underlies these questions; rhetoric which may suit women or the House of Commons, yet whose persuasive powers, so greatly overestimated in our age, cannot suffice to delve into the core of things. But I must disclose my innermost self to you; a peculiarity, a malaise, a malady of the mind possibly, if you are to grasp that I am divided by just such a bridgeless abyss from the literary tasks lying before me as from those which lie behind me and which I hesitate to call my property. So alien do they appear to me. I do not know if I should more admire the intensity of your benevolence or the incredible sharpness of your memory when you once more recall for me the various little plans I carried about with me in those shared days of splendid enthusiasm. I truly had wished to depict the first years of the reign of Henry VIII, our deceased glorious sovereign!

The posthumous memoirs of my grandfather, the Duke of Exeter, on his negotiations with France and Portugal offered me a sort of basis. And in those happy, active days there flowed into me from Sallust, as though through unstopped channels, that cognition of form, that deep, true, inner form which can only be surmised beyond the impediments of rhetorical artifice. Of such form it can no longer be said that it marshals the material, for it permeates it, renders it obsolete and creates poetry and truth at the same time; an interplay of eternal powers, something as magnificent as music and algebra. That was my dearest plan.

What is Man that he creates plans!

I also toyed with other plans. Your gracious letter conjures these up as well: each one sated with a drop of my blood, they dance before me like sad little gnats beside a gloomy wall on which the bright sunlight of those happy days no longer falls.

I wished to decipher the fables and mythical tales left to us by the ancients, and in which painters and sculptors take infinite, unreflecting pleasure as hieroglyphs of some secret, inexhaustible wisdom whose breath I believed I could sense as if through a veil.

I well recall this plan. Behind it lay I know not what sensuous and spiritual desire: like a hunted stag eager for the water I yearned to enter these naked, gleaming bodies, these sirens and dryads, this Narcissus and Proteus, Perseus and Actaeon. I desired to vanish into them and to speak out of them with tongues. I desired. There was so much else I desired. I thought of beginning a collection of

'Apothegms' such as Julius Caesar had penned: you will recall this cited in a letter by Cicero. Here I considered ranging side by side the most noteworthy expressions of thought which I could collect on journeys whilst in commerce with the learned men and sophisticated women of our day, or with certain members of the population or with educated and distinguished persons. I wished to unite with these, fine adages and reflexions from the works of the ancients and the Italians and whatever else I encountered of intellectual gems from books, manuscripts and conversations. Further to these: the arrangement of especially fine festivals and processions, remarkable crimes and cases of mental frenzy, the depiction of the greatest and most characteristic buildings in the Low Countries, in France and Italy and much else besides. The entire opus was then to be entitled "*nosce te ipsum*' (know thyself).

To be brief: the whole of existence at that time appeared to me in a sort of intoxication as one great unity. Spiritual and bodily reality seemed to me to constitute no contradiction, neither did courtly and animal life, art and non-art, solitude and society. In all things I felt nature, in the aberrations of insanity no less than in the extreme refinements of some Spanish ceremonial; in the gaucheness of young peasants no less than in the sweetest allegories. And in all of nature I felt my own self; when I drank deep draughts of foaming lukewarm milk in my hunting lodge, milked by a tousle-haired farm-hand from a mild-eyed cow's udder into a wooden pail, it felt no different from when I sat in the window-seat built into my study and drew in sweet foaming nourishment for the mind from a folio. One thing was like the other: nothing was of lesser degree either in its dreamlike unearthly nature or in bodily power. And so it continued through the entire breadth of life to right and left. Everywhere I stood in the midst of things and was never aware of mere semblance. Or then again, I instinctively sensed everything is a parable and every creature a key to the next, and I truly felt I possessed the power to grasp one after another by its antlers and to unlock with them as many of the others as could be unlocked. This will explain the title I had thought of giving that encyclopedic book.

It may appear as a well ordered plan by divine providence to one who has access to such beliefs, and that my mind must recoil from such swollen presumption into this utter fecklessness and impotence which remains my permanent inner state. Yet such religious concepts have no hold over me. They belong to the cobwebs through which my thoughts shoot into the void while so many of their fellows remain trapped there and come to rest. The mysteries of faith have hardened for me into a sublime allegory which extends over the fields of my life like a radiant rainbow set at a constant distance, ever prepared to recede should it occur to me to hasten there and to wrap myself in the hem of its mantle.

But, my honoured friend, earthly concepts also elude me in similar fashion. How shall I attempt to depict for you these strange mental torments, this swift upward jerk of fruit-laden boughs above my outstretched hands, this receding of murmuring waters before my parched lips?

My case is briefly this: I have totally lost the capacity to think or speak coherently about anything whatsoever.

At first it gradually became impossible for me to discuss a more demanding or general topic and thereby to have recourse to such words as are commonly and casually employed by everyone. I felt an inexplicable malaise in merely uttering the words 'mind', 'soul' or 'body'. I found it inwardly impossible to pronounce any judgement on the affairs at court, the events at parliament or whatever. And this was not because of any possible scruples, for you know my well-nigh frivolous courage and frankness: but rather those abstract words which our tongue must of necessity employ to voice any sort of judgement, fell apart in my mouth like putrid mushrooms. It so happened that I wished to rebuke my four-year-old daughter Katharina Pompilia for a childish lie of which she had been guilty and point out to her the need always to be truthful, whilst the terms which gushed to my mouth assumed such iridescent shades and so intermingled that I was scarcely able to stumble to the end of the sentence, just as if I had felt nausea. And indeed, with pallid face and pressure on my brow, I left the child standing alone, slammed the door behind me, and only felt to some extent restored once on horseback and taking a brisk gallop across lonely pastures.

Gradually this infirmity spread like a corrosive rust. All judgements, even those in everyday domestic conversations normally made in carefree fashion and with unflinching certainty, became so dubious that I had to cease all participation in such conversations. I was filled

with unaccountable anger, which could only be disguised with difficulty, to hear such things as: this affair
ended well or badly for this or that person; Sherrif N.
is a wicked, Preacher T. is a good man; Tenant M. is to
be pitied, his sons are spendthrifts; another man is to be
envied because his daughters are good housekeepers; this
family is on the rise, another is in decline. All this seemed
to me so unprovable, so mendacious, so full of holes as it
is possible to be. My mind impelled me to see all things
which came up in such conversation as uncannily close
at hand; just as I had once seen a piece of skin on my
little finger through a magnifying glass resembling a
fallow field with furrows and hollows. That is how I now
felt about people and their actions. I no longer succeeded
in taking them in with the simplifying glance of habit.
Everything disintegrated for me into parts, the parts into
further parts, and there remained nothing that could be
captured by a concept. Individual words swam about me;
they assumed the aspect of eyes which stared at me and
into which I in turn must stare. They are vortices which
create vertigo when I look down into them, which spin
relentlessly and through which one arrives at emptiness.

I made an effort to rescue myself from this condition
and enter the intellectual sphere of the ancients. I avoided
Plato, for I dreaded the perils of his metaphoric flight. I
thought mostly of keeping faith with Seneca and Cicero.
I hoped to recover health from this harmony of circum-
scribed and ordered concepts. But I was unable to make
the transition to them. These concepts I understood well
enough: I saw their wonderful interplay of relations rise

up before me like magnificent fountains that played with golden orbs. I could hover about them and see how they interchanged in their play; but they were concerned only with each other and the deepest, the most personal part of my thinking remained excluded from their round dance. I was overcome by a feeling of terrible solitude in their midst. I felt as one locked into a garden with nothing but eyeless statues; once again I fled to free open spaces.

Since that time I lead an existence which I fear you will scarcely comprehend; it flows so trivially, so thoughtlessly. It is an existence indeed scarcely to be distinguished from that of my neighbours, my relatives, and most of the landed gentry of this kingdom, and one not entirely lacking in cheerful and inspiring moments. I have some difficulty in suggesting to you wherein these good moments consist; here words let me down once more. For it is something totally nameless and, indeed in all conscience scarcely nameable which in such moments intrudes on me, flooding some aspect of my daily surroundings like a vessel with its superabundance of higher existence. I cannot expect you to understand me without example and I must beg your indulgence for the paltriness of my examples. A watering can, a harrow abandoned in a field, a dog in the sunlight, a humble graveyard, a cripple, a little farmhouse; all this can become the vessel of my revelation. Each one of these objects and a thousand of their kind generally passed over by the eye with utter indifference, can suddenly, at some moment which is not in my power to command, assume for me a sublime and affecting character which lies beyond all words to express. Yes, it may even be the distinctly imagined idea of an absent object which is granted this mysterious privilege of being filled to the brim with that gently yet fast rising tide of divine sensation. It so happened that I recently gave instructions to strew ample doses of poison for the rats in the milk cellars of one of my dairy farms. I rode out towards evening and, as you may imagine, thought no more about the matter. Then, whilst riding at walking pace over the deeply furrowed field with nothing close by other than a brood of quail put to flight, and in the distance the great sun setting over undulating fields, there suddenly opened up within me this cellar, crammed with the death-throes of that race of rats. Everything was within me: the cool musty cellar air filled with the sickly pungent smell of the poison and the high-pitched death-screams echoing from mouldering walls; those fiercely embroiled spasms of impotence, hectic flights of criss-crossing despair; maddened search for escape; the cold look of rage when two met at a blocked-off cranny. But what good is my searching for words again which I have forsworn! Do you recall, my friend, that marvellous description from Livy of the hours that precede the destruction of Alba Longa? How they stray through the streets which they are never to see again . . . how they take leave of the stones on the ground. I tell you, my friend, I carried this within me and the burning of Carthage too; but it was something beyond that, it was more divine, more bestial, and it was the present, the fullest, most sublime present. There was a mother who had her dying young in spasms around her and who directed her glances not at those who were dying, not at the pitiless stone walls, but at the empty air, or through the air into infinity, and accompanied these glances with a gnashing of teeth! – When a dutiful slave stood close by the stiffening body of Niobe, filled with impotent terror, he must have gone through what I went through, as within me this animal soul bared its teeth in defiance of that monstrous fate.

You must forgive me this description and should not think that it was pity that filled me. You ought not to think that on any account, otherwise my example was clumsily chosen. It was far more and far less than pity: a tremendous form of sympathy, an outpouring of the self into these creatures or else a sensation that an effusion of life and death, of dreaming and waking, had for an instant passed over into them – but from where? For what had this to do with pity, what with intelligible human thought-connection, if on yet another evening I find a half-filled watering-can beneath a nut tree, left behind by a gardener's apprentice. The water in it is darkened by the shade of the tree and a water-beetle scuttles across the surface of this water from one dark shore to another; if this coincidence of trivia thrills me with such a powerful sense of the infinite, thrills me from the roots of my hair to the very marrow of my heels, that I wish to break out in words which I know, were I to find them, would force to earth the very cherubim in whom I do not believe. Then I turn away in silence from that spot and weeks later, when I catch a glimpse of that nut tree, I pass by with a timid sidelong glance since I do not wish to dispel that lingering sense of the marvellous which still haunts the stem, nor dispel the greater than earthly raptures which continue to pulsate about the bushes close by. At such moments an insignificant creature, a dog, a rat, a beetle, a withered apple tree, a cart-track snaking over a hill, a moss-covered stone, means more to me than the loveliest, most adoring lover in a blissful night had ever meant. These dumb and sometimes inanimate creatures reach out towards me with such plenitude, such deep presence of love, that my fervent eye can scarcely find a spot that is dead. Everything, simply everything in existence, everything I recall, everything touched on by most confused thoughts appears to me to have being. Even my own heaviness, the recurrent dullness of my brain, seem to hold significance; I feel a delightful, essentially infinite interplay of opposites within and about me, and among all the contending bodies there is none which I might not enter. It appears then as if my body consisted of endless ciphers which can unlock all things for me. Or it is as if we could enter upon a new, mysterious relationship with all existence once we had begun to think with our heart. Yet once this strange, trance-like state vanishes, I can give no real account of it; I am then no more capable of representing in rational terms what this whole world-embracing harmony consisted in and how it communicated itself to me, than I could give a precise account of the internal motions of my entrails or the stemming of the flow in my bloodstream.

Apart from these strange coincidences which, by the way, I scarcely know whether to attribute to mind or body, I live a life of almost unbelievable emptiness and have difficulty in disguising this inner paralysis from my wife and this indifference from members of my staff who remind me of the affairs involving the estate. The good, strict upbringing which I owe to my father, and the early acquired habit of leaving no hour of the day unused are, it seems to me, the sole reason for preserving sufficient outward control over my life and the appearance appropriate to my standing and person.

I am rebuilding a wing of my house and can bring myself now and then to speak with the architect about the progress of his work; I manage my estates and my tenants and officials will likely find me more laconic but no less amiable than before. Not one among them standing in his doorway with doffed cap when I ride by in the evening will have an inkling that my glance, which he is wont to catch respectfully, is searching with longing beyond the decaying timbers under which he is used to search for angler's bait; my glance which plunges through the narrow, grated window into the stuffy chamber where the low bedstead with coloured linen in the corner ever seems to await someone who is to die or someone about to be born. Who is to know that my glance lingers on the ugly whelps or the cat which lithely slips through the flower-pots, and that amongst all these paltry and cumbersome objects of peasant life it is seeking for that unique thing whose inconspicuous form, whose wholly unremarked lying or leaning there, whose dumb essence may become the source of that mysterious, wordless, boundless rapture. For my unnamed feeling of bliss will sooner break forth from some distant, lonely shepherd's fire, than from the sight of the starry heavens, sooner from the chirp of a last dying cricket once the autumn wind drives wintry clouds across the empty fields, than from the majestic roll of an organ. At times I compare myself in thought with Crassus, that orator of whom it is reported that he grew so immeasurably fond of a tame moray, a dull, red-eyed, dumb fish in his ornamental pond, that it became the talk of the city. And when Domitius once reproached him before the Senate with having shed tears over this fish's death, and thereby attempted to make him appear halfway a fool, Crassus made him the reply: "Then at the death of my fish, I did what you failed to do at the death of either your first or your second wife."

I do not know how often this Crassus and his moray springs to mind as the mirror-image of my own self, bridging the abyss of centuries. But not on account of the reply he gave to Domitius. The reply brought the laughs over on his side so that the affair was resolved in a joke. Yet the affair touches me closely; this affair would have remained the same even if Domitius had wept tears of blood in sincerest grief for his wives. For Crassus would still stand confronting him with his tears for his moray. And it is on this figure, whose ludicrous banality amidst a world-governing Senate debating the loftiest issues is so glaringly apparent, on this figure some mysterious impulse compels me to reflect in a way that seems perfectly foolish, the instant I attempt to express it in words.

Sometimes the image of this Crassus lodges in my brain at night like a splinter about which everything festers, pulsates and boils. It seems then as if I myself were to ferment, to form blisters, to seethe and to sparkle. The whole thing is a kind of feverish thinking, but thinking within a material which is more immediate, more liquid, more glowing than words. They are equally vortices, yet not such as the vortices of language, which seem to lead into a bottomless void, but somehow into myself and into the deepest domain of peace.

I have pestered you unduly, my honoured friend, with this expansive depiction of an inexplicable condition which usually remains concealed within me.

You were so kind as to express your disappointment at the fact that no book published by me reaches you any longer, "to compensate you for the renouncement of my company". At this moment I feel with a certainty, not unmixed with a measure of attendant pain, that I shall also not be writing a book in English or Latin within the coming year and in all subsequent years of my life; and this for the sole reason that I leave this irksome aberration to your infinite intellectual superiority to establish its place without prejudice within your harmoniously ordered realm of spiritual and physical phenomena: and this because the language in which it might have been possible for me to write or think, is neither Latin, nor English, nor Italian and Spanish, but a language of which no single word is known to me, a language in which voiceless things speak to me and in which I may perhaps one day render account in my grave before an unknown judge. I wish it were given to me to compress into the last words of this in all probability last letter that I write to Francis Bacon, all the love and gratitude, the boundless admiration that I harbour in my heart for the greatest benefactor of my mind, for the foremost Englishman of my time, and will continue to harbour until it breaks in death.

A.D. 1603, this 22nd August.
Phi. Chandos

APPENDIX: SELECT POEMS BY LORIS

AN EXPERIENCE

The twilit vale was quite suffused
With mists of silver grey, as when the moon
Filters through clouds. And yet it was not night.
My dimly fading thoughts merged
With the misty silver-grey of the dark vale,
And silently I sank beneath the surging
Transparent sea and left this life.
What wondrous flowers appeared,
Calyxes darkly gleaming. A wilderness of plants
Through which yellow-red light, topaz-like,
Pulsed in warm streams and glowed. The whole
Replete with a deep swelling sound
Of melancholy music. And this I knew,
Though grasp it I could not, and yet I knew:
Death is at hand. He has turned into music,
Mighty and yearning, sweet and darkly gleaming,
Kindred to deepest melancholy.

Yet strange!
A nameless yearning for life
Wept silently within my soul, wept
As one must weep who passes by
His town on dark blue waters,
His father's town, on some great ocean ship
With giant yellow sails towards eventide.
There he sees narrow streets, hears fountains playing,

Smells fragrance of the lilac trees, sees himself,
A child beside the shore, with a child's eyes,
Timid and on the verge of tears, sees in his room
Light through an open window -
But the great ocean ship bears him along
Gliding in silence upon deep blue waters
With giant yellow sails all strangely formed.

YOUR COUNTENANCE

Your countenance was overcast with dreams.
Silent, I gazed at you in mute alarm.
How memories rose! That I had once
In former nights delivered up my inmost self
Both to the moon and that too dearly loved vale,
Upon whose barren slopes there stood apart
Some haggard trees and in between
Those lower little wisps of cloud adrift

And through the stillness yet, the ever fresh
And ever strange white silvery waters
The stream gave gushing forth – how memories rose!

How memories rose! For to these many things
And to their beauty – fruitless as it was -
I wholly gave myself with keenest longing,
As I do now with gazing on your hair
And through your eyelids that deep gleam!

THE MAIDEN AND DEATH

This green and liquid gold is poison and it kills.
How sweet it smells: as though the hectic wind
Had wildly tangled in acacia trees,
As one treads silently by moonlight on soft blossoms …
Perhaps the state of death is just such soundless motion
Through strange and vacant countries without sleep,
Across mute bridges spanning waters green
Through long black speechless avenues,
Through gardens that grow wild …
At last I come upon the House of Death:
In the great hall a giant table stands
Of deep green malachite which gryphons bear.
There Death is seated, who invites me
And hosts of pages with fine slender hands
And shoes of satin black with soundless tread.
These now serve up most wondrous dishes:
Indeed, whole peacocks, fish with silver scales
And scarlet fins, in whose fine teeth
(They are all gilded) sprigs of laurel lodge
And grapes of gold-red rust and open
Pomegranates that gleam upon soft cushions
Of fresh violets, and Death is clothed
In a mantle of white satin
And bids me sit beside him
And is most genteel

SERENE HOUSE

Upon an open balcony heavenward sang
An aged man upon an organ playing,
Whilst at his feet, upon the threshing-floor,
The slender with the bearded grandson vied,
That through the flawless oleander stem
A tremor upwards passed; and yet a bird
Silent within its crown's full-flowering sheen
Did not fly off but earthwards eyed with knowing glance
And sitting on the well's rough-hewn rim
The young woman suckled her child.

Only the Wanderer, whose road lay
On past threshing-floor and round its walls,
Did cast a stranger's backward glance
And bore away – kin to that evening cloud
Drifting afar past silent stream and wood -
That wondrous image of tranquillity.

BEFORE DAYBREAK

Now fitful lies along the pallid rim of sky
The thunderstorm sunk in upon itself
Now thinks the sick man: 'Daylight! I can go to sleep!'
And closes his hot eyelids. Now the young stabled cow
Puts forth her avid nostrils
Towards cool morning odours. Now in the silent forest
The vagrant rises unwashed
From his soft bed of last year's leaves
And with an idle hand launches the nearest stone
At the odd pigeon flying by drowsy with sleep,
Then senses dread as the stone falls
Muffled and heavily to earth. Now water darts
As if it thought to hasten after night, by now advanced,
Into the dark, all heedless, wild
And with chill breath, whilst overhead
The Saviour and His Mother, softly, softly
Confer upon the little bridge: softly,
And yet their little words are everlasting
And indestructible like yonder stars.
He bears His Cross and only says: 'My Mother!'
And looks at her, and: 'Oh, my beloved Son!'
She says. – Now sky and earth
Hold dumb, oppressive intercourse. Then runs a shudder
Through the heavy, ancient body:
She readies herself to live the coming day.
Now there awakes the phantom light of dawn. Now
Someone slips unshod out of a woman's bed,
Flits like a shadow, clambers like a thief

Through the window into his own room, sees
Himself in the wall-mirror and is gripped by fear
In face of this pale, sleep-starved stranger,
As though this man had last night murdered
The kindly boy, his former self,
And now came but to wash his hands,
As if in scorn, in this his victim's little jug,
And therefore was the sky so bleak
And all the air so strangely filled.
Now creaks the stable door. Now day has come.

WHAT IS THIS WORLD?

What is this world? An everlasting lay,
From which the godhead's spirit shines and glows,
From which the wine of wisdom foams and flows,
And then to us the sound of love conveys
And all our inner changing ways,
It is a shaft of light fed by the sun,
A line of verse with thousands interspun,
Which fades unheeded, wastes, decays.

HE AND SHE

The cup she carried in her hand,
Her chin and mouth reflect its round –
So light and steadfast was her tread,
No drop out of the cup was shed.

So light the sureness of his hand:
He rode upon a youthful horse,
And with a gesture, scorning force,
He brought it to a quivering stand.

And yet in reaching for the hand
Which would this light cup have bestowed,
The burden proved for both too great,
For both, in trembling, knew a state
Where neither hand its partner found,
And so to earth the dark wine flowed.

Translator Alexander Stillmark, who graduated in Modern Languages at Jesus College Cambridge, is Emeritus Reader in German at University College London. A comparative literary scholar and a leading specialist in Austrian Studies, he has published widely on nineteenth and twentieth century topics. His translations both from and into German include: GEORG TRAKL: POEMS AND PROSE (London, 2001, Evanston Illinois, 2005); GEDICHTE IN PROSA VON DER ROMANTIK BIS ZUR JAHRHUNDERTWENDE (Frankfurt am Main, 2013); HUGO VON HOFMANNSTHAL, AN IMPOSSIBLE MAN (Cambridge, 2016); and ADALBERT STIFTER, TALES OF OLD VIENNA AND OTHER PROSE (Riverside, California, 2016). He has twice been awarded a translation prize by the Federal Chancellor's Bureau, Austria. Forthcoming: a translation with Introduction of Hugo von Hofmannsthal's last comedy, THE INCORRUPTIBLE SERVANT.